I Wrote a Book About You

Amy Louise Ware

Amy Louise Ware is a part time cover teacher, author and puppy Mumma. She is in her third year of an English Language and Literature Degree with The Open University, and lives in Cheshire. *I Wrote A Book About You* is her first romantic comedy novel.

I Wrote a Book About You
Amy Louise Ware

Cover photographed by Tracey Joanne Ware
(AKA my Mum, thanks Mum)
Cover edited by yours truly

Special thanks...

To all of my lovely editors (and guinea pigs) for my first EVER rom com novel.

A very big thank you to my very patient Mother, my big sister Laura and Tom, my legendary and soon to be brother in law. Thank you to Dave Lane a dear friend, Georgia (your brutally honest humour inspired one of my favourite characters), Zoe (who had sweaty palms reading my big twists), Dymphna (couldn't go amiss with that name), Sophie Smith (for her ongoing bath time readership), Vicky Haslam, Natalie Tompkins, Lauren Kerry and of course my adopted big bro Rob Simpson.

Also, a huge thanks to Nicole Strange for her constant feedback on how to improve this book – she pushed me to keep editing and crafting this story.

To Tupper, my crazy nutjob of a puppy, who provided endless cuddles and managed to persuade me to make him into a character! You'll soon find out who!

To all of those who read the initial preview of my book and left a review too. You guys were unbelievably helpful: Bobby Buchanan, Emily Hart, Richard Gregson, Carole Thomas, Nicole Strange, Natasha Gurr, Rebekah Hindle, Angie Bee, Vicky Haslam and Zoe Smith.

To my Blurb editors, Helen Sehne, Alison Kaye, Sadie Johnson, Jessica Field and David Few – thank you.

Working with you all has been an absolute dream. Love you guys.

To John Stead and Andy McMorine for your first-hand dyslexia experience, that helped me to fully portray its effect on different people's lives.

To all the heartbreakers and various knob heads who inspired some characters in this book. Thanks a lot guys, much appreciated.

To the future guy that I am going to fall in love with. Just know, I wrote a book about you in advance. And I hope that's ok.

To 'Made in Chelsea' – thank you for keeping me sane for the two years that I was writing this novel. On Monday nights, I'd stay up until midnight multitasking: watching TV, writing, and stroking Tupper. Singleton life. I'm officially a hoot.

To Joanne Richards at *Choc A Doodle Doo*, AKA the best sweet shop in the land, for helping me to promote this novel. Also, to *The Effective Directories* for helping me to promote my book!

Oh, and just as a side note to all those writers out there who keep getting knocked down and told their work isn't good enough. Don't ever give up. You're fab. And one day, we writers are going to run the world with our amazing fictional characters. Okay?

For Dad, and Jake

I wrote this book for you – and by you, I mean the invented fictional guy in this book, whom I am still waiting to find.
He seems to be bloody lost right now...

Chapter 1

POSY

Introducing Me

Did he know where I was? Did he even care? I don't think he did – at least that's what I told myself every day when I woke up to see an empty bedside. It's so crazy how you can go from being so intimate with someone one minute to blocking them off your Instagram or Facebook.

The linen sheets were cool upon my naked skin and slipped into the creases of my body like chocolate oozing into perfectly shaped molds. Come to think of it, the only chocolate molds I've ever owned are penis shaped - a wedding gift from my nutjob of a best friend, Jodie. But I'll tell you more about her later.

I had spent my early twenties teaching high

schoolers and loved every single minute of it. I regularly embarrassed myself and the kids - my most memorable moment being when I accidentally locked myself and thirty of my Year 9s in a classroom by accident. I'd panicked and tried to yank the door open, and one of my newly stuck on false nails went flying off into the air, hitting a student in the eye, who then had to be airlifted to hospital.

Safe to say I now always carry nail glue. In fact, as a joke every year Jodie always buys me nail glue so I never cause another child to be airlifted. She's funny like that.

Anyway, after leaving my teaching job in a high school in Kent, which I truly did adore, I spent the next ten months attempting to travel the world like Liz Gilbert in *Eat, Pray Love*. Instead, I'd ended up in France, Austria and Ireland. I finished my year's 'travelling' in Barcelona, my personal favourite out of them all - which is where this story begins.

I'd intended on exploring the whole world as a child; always making myself paper planes and pretending that I would one day be onboard one, travelling to the likes of Macchu Pichu, spending a year with a tribe of naked Native Indians or perhaps waking up with someone in a tent, to watch the sun rise and set on The Great Wall of China.

Speaking of camping, I had tried to persuade my

Mum to camp with me once but she had refused and said (and these are her words entirely) "I am not going to shit in a hole darling or use a *shared* shower. Do you want me to get chlamydia?"

Mothers.

Those plans of being a cultured traveller well and truly went tits up when my now ex-husband decided to run off with one of his apprentices a year ago, and take our entire bank account with him.

My ex-husband was a lawyer, he knew the system – I wanted an amicable split, he wanted to make sure that I knew that without him, I was in fact worth nothing. My friend Jodie refuses to refer to him with any other name but knobwank nowadays. Quite rightly so.

~

That summer, I was lying lazily on my Spanish mattress which was propped up on bricks and it was surprisingly comfy. It was just like having constant acupuncture; you didn't dare move but after a while it felt good. The Barcelona sun had always peeked through the window every morning, shining down across that bedside where his body used to be all those years ago, and the sunshine was gladly welcomed every single day, unlike him.

The sun tinted my skin, it made my nose glow and

my shoulders shimmer.

The sunshine is 'Hermosa' so they say; I first remember hearing that word down by the marina in Barcelona. A young Papa described his child as being hermosa. With my blondness, tendency to daydream, and obsession with food, I thought he was talking about samosas at first, but overtime I've learnt about a very magical thing known as Google Translate, and I'm getting a little better with my, err... Española!

Beautiful, that sunshine was. As beautiful as that small girl sat beside me on the marina that day. Her eyes, blue, were as piercing and as mesmerizing as the ocean, and her skin golden, glistening like the sand. Her ears were pierced and she wore her hair in two buns on top of either side of her head, and with small ringlets falling behind each ear.

The small girl I am describing is one of the many reasons I fell head over heels for Spain. The day that I saw her on the marina was on the afternoon of the morning I had arrived, and I was captivated by how loved she was. It juxtaposed my own unloved feeling following recent events and it healed me somehow. I fell for the culture because of the pure beauty of it.

Beauty is hard to find these days. Heartbreak on the other hand, well, it's as common as a cold.

~

I don't know how I hadn't guessed earlier, I never suspected the guy I'd loved since I was seventeen to become the man I would marry, the man I would love, and the man I would eventually find with another woman's panties in his top drawer. When I confronted him about the underwear, he said he'd bought them for me and that he wasn't 'screwing another chick'. As a friend of mine always says, cheaters will go to incredible lengths to hide their affair. I guess the pants in his drawer were a major slip up because it could have been the moment I discovered he was cheating, but he convinced me otherwise with his sly and persuasive lies. Hamilton had this way of making you believe anything he said; he had me wrapped around his finger whilst he was screwing someone else.

Yes, Hamilton (the ex hubby) was a fan of the ladies, and an even bigger fan of the female anatomy. It's taken me a whole year to be able to curse his name, without feeling guilty.

After the first few months following the divorce I kept reanalyzing my decision to divorce him. Was it me and not him? Had I caused the fling he had because I wasn't around? Or was it all just in my head?

Then I thought, fuck it, he's the one in the wrong for putting his dick where he shouldn't have. Gosh,

I am turning into Jodie, my best friend, more and more with my frequent expletives. Heartbreak changes you.

After a year of so-called travelling I can answer every single one of those questions. Hamilton was, is, and will forever be a knob and that's not my fault... it's his parents', right? I didn't make him after all... I bet that sperm is regretting its little venture to the eggs-directory.

I never imagined I'd become the stronger person, but I did. I felt like a new woman. A new, twenty-six-year-old, single woman. Still younger than ever. Or so I kept telling myself – though I was pretty sure I had seen a grey hair *down there* whilst in Barcelona, I mean what the... fuzz. Where are my tweezers at?

~

I forced myself to emerge from my bricky, Barcelonian bed and peeled the covers away from my midriff. I pushed the linen aside and turned my legs to the edge of the bed, dangling my feet like Dad and I used to do when we would go crabbing on the Island.

Dad had taught me to dip my toes in the water, and to dive in, no life vest – though I must say, my dive is much more widely described, by dictionary definition, as a full-on belly flop. I am not graceful whatsoever, but I embrace it. Also, don't dive in if it's shark infested waters because that wouldn't exactly end well. You might not have any toes to dip into the water if you do...

I leant across to the bedside table, turned on my radio and thought – what other way to wake up than with a song? John Mayer erupted from the speakers at the touch of a button and as always, his voice was gladly welcomed.

I stretched my arms up above my head, making sleepy flamenco movements with my hands to the sexy and sweet serenade, then joined my hands together, making a slightly orgasmic, satisfactory noise.

I hoped Augustina next door hadn't heard me. She was forever banging on (excuse the expression) about me missing out on what her husband gives her. Seriously, Augustina was sixty-seven-years-old, and the walls were as thin as toilet paper that your fingers slide through. I heard everything. And I mean the whole sha-BANG.

I placed my feet on the warmed-by-the-Barcelonian-sunshine marbled floor and wandered into the kitchen, swaying to the music as I went.
Though not completely elegantly as I stubbed my toe on the edge of the kitchen table and yelled out, "Shit. Fuck. Shit!"

It wasn't exactly the type of kitchen you'd see in IKEA, but it did the job – I mean, I wasn't ever starving, which is always a positive, right?

I dreaded having to leave Barcelona because I'd fallen in love with it, but I knew that when I got home I wouldn't miss it - I didn't get attached anymore.

I guess Hamilton (from now on to be referred to as Dick because frankly I'm feeling hormonal, and well, the name suits him) has a lot to do with my impermanence, my hesitance and my lack of trust in men. When I left him and began my travels, I was probably 1% (tops) myself, and on the day I'm referring to, I was probably 99.9% me. It was just that 0.1% that was missing, and I wasn't quite sure what it is.

Suddenly being a divorced woman at twenty-five has a way of dropping you right in the deep end. You're at that time in your life when you want a mature man, but all the good ones are taken. So instead the only penises you see are on Spanish subtitled reruns of *Embarrassing Bodies*.

Twenty-five is also the age when you're watching everyone else get knocked up (but not in an unplanned kind of way). I mean, my Nana used to always ring up and ask when I was going to give her some grandchildren as if they just grow on trees.

My reply? *Well Nana, when there's an option to impregnate oneself I will let you know.*

So, there I was, younger than ever, thinking I'd be happily married for the rest of my life to my high school sweetheart. How cliché that he ran off with another woman younger than him and twice his size – she might as well have been in high school.

But when I walked out on Hamilton a lot of people walked into my life – my crazy family and friends.

My family isn't too big, but it isn't too small either, it's just right - I wonder where I got my inspiration from there?

I've got the typical Mum and Dad who've been rocky, a totally awesome half brother Noah, his wife Izzy and their two kiddos.

My half-brother, Noah, is the definition of perfect. Always on time, a smooth talker, no reason not to like him. He was there for me throughout the heartbreaks pre-Hamilton, during-Hamilton and post-Hamilton, and has stuck by my side until this day.

Noah was always the Ross Gellar type, constantly droning on about T-Rex's, raving about the most recent Dinosaur books, or zoning into NASA TV every Thursday evening. He was the geeky one and I was the utter nutcase with henna tattoos everywhere (needles aren't my thing), and wacky blonde and pink hair.

The back story of Noah's conception is pretty interesting so listen up and grab a notepad, because this is *quite* the story.

Noah had never met his paternal Dad. Mum said it had been a one-night stand in her hippie stage, with a younger man. She didn't even know his name, or so that's what she had said at the time. She hadn't loved him. She'd slept with him in an attempt to make my Dad jealous, who was her on-off boyfriend at the time.

We have a difficult and complicated family, so keep up.

Mum never got the chance to tell Noah's real Dad about his existence as she left the morning after, without uttering a word, and told me that even if she'd have had the chance to tell him, she wouldn't have.

My Mum is pretty stubborn in that way. She's an independent soul, but sometimes her independence pushes people away.

The one-night stand with Noah's Dad resulted in her pregnancy, because, shall we say, he didn't glove his baby making device. For years, *my* Dad was convinced Noah was his kid.

Mum kept the truth a secret. God knows how she did it.

If you know anyone that knows me, they will tell you I am the worst liar on the planet. You wouldn't want me as your lawyer, let's put it that way.

But when Noah got a little older and looked seemingly more and more like the guy my Mum had had a fling with, Dad started questioning what Mum did *that* summer - and so the truth came out.

Mum finally cracked like a teapot dropped onto marble floor.

Cutting a long story short, there was a near divorce, but then all was forgiven and Mum and Dad now live happily running a B&B in Surrey. Dad treats Noah as his son which is lovely, and as an outsider you'd be clueless about the truth because Dad and Noah have the exact same mannerisms, just completely different looks.

When I reached my teenage years, I did start to resent my Mum... I don't think I could keep a secret so big from the one I loved. I guess you could say that in that way I'm pretty stubborn too. It takes a lot for me to change my opinion about something. Don't get me wrong I get on with my Mum, but Dad is my first point of call. Dad just gets me. And to be honest, not many people do.

Going back to my brother, Noah was always the favoured child, and I was always the imperfect one – the one under CIA monitoring at those compulsory family meals, in case any blasphemous words cascaded from my big mouth. Funny how I befriended Jodie who's also got a big, blasphemous mouth, perhaps more so than me!

It was Noah who always looked after me when I was a tiddlywink – in fact, it was Noah who persuaded me to venture out of our little town after my divorce. He told me if I didn't, I would either a) end up marrying a guy that didn't deserve me, or b) turn into one of those weird cat ladies. And I'm allergic to cats so that would be really, really crappo.

My big brother married Izzy – who's a Doctor – at 21, and they had their first child at 22. They did it all the 'right way'. Though by my calculation, my nephew Niall was a little early being born... Hmmm... Golden child not so much eh Noah?

I love being an Aunty. It's kind of like that advantage of buying a dress that you can return; if the kids start kicking off and throwing Cheerios at each other, they're not yours, so you can just pass them back to their rightful owners.

Don't get me wrong, I love kids, but I wouldn't want to have them with a guy just for the sake of proving to my Nana that I'm not asexual. And after all, it's unlikely I could ever conceive, but that's between me and you. I'll tell you about it later.

I have one nephew, Niall (the one who was obviously a little earlier than planned...) and one niece, Jessie. I love them to bits. So, for now, those guys are my practice run for when I do have a bun in the oven.

Emphasis on the *when* there. In fact, I didn't even have an oven in my apartment in Barcelona. More like a bun in the microwave. Eugh, the waitress wage.

~

Flicking on the coffee machine, the smell of caffeine filled the kitchen and pleased my senses. Morning coffee was my daily wake up treat. Who needs a man when they have coffee? At least coffee tastes nice when it's in your mouth...

In Spain, coffee is considered to be more important than food itself. And I've got to say, it beats most men too. Coffee doesn't demand sex. Coffee doesn't hurt you. And coffee is always waiting for you in the morning when you wake up, but not many men are - I can tell you that from experience.

Taking my freshly brewed coffee, I grabbed a banana from the fruit bowl and a Magdalena that was staring me down on top of the bread bin, and made my way out onto the terrace.

Placing myself down on one of the chairs, I rested my bare feet on the warm table-top as the sunrays rose from the East. What a view. Barcelona was so quiet beneath me; it was a strange place but so beautiful too. The culture was the total opposite to my home, but I liked it. At 6am I could already hear the seagulls flying above me and the erupting quietness of the sleepy hustle and bustle cascading from the stoned streets.

I heard a buzz coming from within the kitchen and dragged my sleepy feet to retrieve it. I nearly dropped my phone with the excitement of what I read.

Hey foxy lady, I'm in Barcelona nxt week with work, could I stay with u pleeeaassseeee! I have concert tickets... and many other bribes if u try and say no to my amazing company you sexy bitch.
Love you nutcase.
Love Jodie
(AKA fellow nutcase)
xx
p.s. are you having lots of rampant sex with a Spanish señor as we speak?

It's odd how much you begin to miss what you know when you move away from home. Jodie and I have been friends from the very beginning – she has been there for me since puberty (which was a long time ago) through the troubled teenage years when I decided to dye my hair yellow, the Hamilton years (including the engagement), the marriage and the consequent divorce, and life even to this day.

Jodie is a solicitor who works for an international real estate firm; she's always flying out here there and everywhere – and it's not often our travelling paths cross.

So, when they rarely do, I turn into crazy-nutcase-friend mode and splurge on the necessities:

1. *Popcorn*
2. *Scary movies*
3. *Wine*
4. *Tissues*
5. *Oreos*
6. *More wine and whisky... Jodie likes whisky, oooohhh and hot chocolate*

Whilst multitasking, writing down my girly week shopping list and stuffing a Magdalena down my throat, I texted Jodie back.

Yo sister from another mister. Yes yes yes. Please. I could do with some company before I leave in a few weeks. Writing down shopping list

**essentials as we speak. Love and miss you.
Gonna go shower now because I'm a dirty girl
lol. Posy xxxx
p.s. and no, I am officially a practicing
mermaid. Legs glued shut involuntarily babe!**

I chuckled to myself as I finished constructing my text. Concluding my last mouthful of Magdalena and coffee, I clicked send and headed for a shower, throwing off my dressing gown onto my bed in a very unrehearsed, unsexy strip show kind of way. I was pretty hot, so a cold shower it was. Before climbing in, I paused to catch myself in the mirror - my little post-breakfast food baby making an appearance.

Note to self: I should probably stop eating 'Party Rings' and low fat 'Jammie Dodgers' for breakfast.

Then I heard a ding from within the shower which made me jump, I thought it must be a Facebook notification – after all, Jodie wouldn't text back that quick. It usually takes her a week tops to reply to any message. The water was trickling along the curves of my shoulders and down the edges of my shoulder blades when I heard someone knocking.

Shit. Shit balls.

I quickly grabbed a towel and put one foot out of the shower, but there was water on the floor that had leaked from the crappy pipes and I went flying into the air, landing flat bang on my bum, my legs spread eagle – and not in a satisfactory way.

I rubbed my sore bum and quickly grabbed my dressing gown from the door knob to cover my nakedness. I thought how lovely it would be to see Jodie soon, whilst on my way to answer the door.

After all, what better way to spend my last few weeks in Spain than with no one other than my best friend?

I reached the door and fumbled around with the locks made for someone as talented as Houdini to undo. Yes, voila! It opened.

And guess who was standing there screaming the entire apartment block down?

Jodie.

"Surprise sexy lady!" she screamed.

"But... how... what... OH MY GOD YOU'RE HERE... NOW! I'm... I'm ... Naked, actually!" I blurted out and chuckled to myself, a huge belly laugh erupting from us both.

And Jodie, being the friend that Jo is, tugged on my towel as we were greeting each other with a huge hug – and within seconds I was stood stark naked outside my own apartment. Talk about making sure the neighbors remember who you are. We both burst out laughing. It was going to be a fun few weeks – I could feel it.

Jodie's the type of friend who will fart in the cubicle next to you and then shout out, "Aww babe, you gotta cut down on those onions or at least take an Imodium!!"

Yeah that type of friend. The one you want to kill sometimes.

Jodie and I spent the evening talking on and on about the gossip back in Kent. Jodie and I grew up together, went through the heartbreaks together, but the difference was that Jodie was a single woman by choice, and I wasn't. We drowned ourselves in extra-large glasses of wine and pathetically cried on each other's shoulders watching a late-night re-run of *Marley & Me*, in Spanish. We even cried without the fucking audio. Dogs dying are a no-go for me and Jo.

We had slowly gone through the wine stages – it started off with the giggly stage where you laugh at ANYTHING, then the zoning out stage, and then the serious "are you sure you're not lonely?" area.
I remember when I was about seventeen, my Mum treated me to my first glass of wine whilst we were out one summer afternoon and I showed up at my Nana's in full on giggly mode. Oooppsss.

The wine brought up conversations of the past, of times when we had both been happier than we were in that moment.

Jodie asked me if I had heard from Hamilton as she'd seen him in the supermarket back home, he'd been with another woman whom she'd heard him calling something along the lines of Bel, Bella or Squishy (VOM) – obviously not the same one he'd run off with when he decided to turn our already unhappy marriage into shreds.

The truth was, I hadn't heard from Hamilton since the day I walked out of that house. His lawyer had contacted me, but Hamilton had wiped me off his chalkboard and replaced me with a shiny new one, with fake boobs to go with it.

Jodie asked me something I hadn't ever considered that night which was, "Do you still love him?"

A tear fell down my face as I contemplated the sheer reality of my life in that moment.

"No," I said. "I think what I miss the most is what could have been... I, I miss what we had planned to do together, but the thought of him ever laying a hand upon me again – no, I don't miss that. I actually resent the fact that I let him have a hold on me for so long. Missing him is the last thing on my mind."

Jodie pushed a strand of my hair behind my ear and gently rested her head on my shoulder. A gesture where no words were needed.

I smiled to myself after a while and said, "Though, if I'm being honest – I do miss sex. Not with him because it was like a ride at Alton Towers that desperately needed renovating. But, I think if I don't find someone soon it's going to dry up like a desert down there!"

"Well when's the last time you, you know?" asked Jodie cheekily.

"Ha-ha a few weeks ago with this wanker of a guy called Alfie Dalton. He was good though, he knew what buttons to press on my ride."

And within moments Jodie and I had gone from the serious wine stage right back into full on giggle mode.
We then began discussing how I'd found a grey hair down below, and then Jodie, being very nearly off her face on Shiraz went into the bathroom to inspect her own belongings for peace of mind! What else are friends for, right?

Chapter 2

POSY

Rain, rain don't go away

After a lovely and frankly drunken evening with Jodie, we spent the next day mooching around the Barcelona architecture, being total geeks and taking various selfies next to the most beautiful places you'll ever see. Jodie mostly sticking her two fingers up behind my head whenever she had the chance too. Jodie the Joker.

From 2pm to 7pm I was waitressing, so Jodie said she would go back to the apartment and make some tea before the concert. Her challenge was to produce something magnificent with a... microwave.

Jodie had texted me about the concert tickets and

quite frankly I could not wait for my shift to be over. Serving coffee to miserable old Spanish men or jumping up and down in a seriously sweaty bubble of dancing people – I must say I was more swayed towards the latter. A night out was a rare occasion for me who usually was in bed for 11pm to catch a rerun of *Homes Under the Hammer.*

At 7pm I clocked off work and practically sprinted like Usain Bolt back to the apartment. Jodie had cooked up an absolute storm. Chickpea burgers with a barbecue dressing and an avocado side salad. It screamed EAT ME, not literally though.

I was surprised; Jodie had never been able to cook, she was more of a basic baked beans on toast kind of gal. I stared at her in shock and inquired "WOW! When did you become Nigella?", and then she chuckled.

"What? What is it? Do I have something on my face?" I asked smiling.

"No no you don't, it's just, well…" Jodie began guiltily, "I ordered it all from the Mexican café down the road and then put in onto your plates to make it look like I can cook. I'm happy to take credit for it though!" she said, laughing.

I laughed out loud, "Who do you think you are Mrs. Doubtfire?"

Jodie then creased over absolutely wetting her knickers, after singing 'Dude Looks Like a Lady' in reply to me, with the hoover movement included. We are as nutty as they come.

We enjoyed our feast, then began getting ready for the concert. Jodie begged to do my makeup as she'd seen a picture of Jessica Alba in Cosmopolitan on her flight over and she said her look would just look *'fucking fabulous'* on me.

Though in reality, I knew she'd make me look like an A-Class hooker.

After yanking my ripped jeans on and my "I Really Like the Stones" tee, I threw on a pair of pink Converse and we were ready to go out of the door.

"So, who's concert are we going to?" I asked as we climbed aboard the local shuttle, which was bustling with the locals on their way to their own destinations.

Jodie scrunched up her fists with obvious excitement, "They're called *The Rainer's*, and guess what? I just so happen to be selling their band manager a huge estate here in Barcelona sooooo that means we get to go to the AFTER PARTAYYYY!".

I squealed with excitement, like a new Mum on her first night out in months. I deserved a night out.

Who knows, maybe I'd even meet someone super nice and the opposite of what I usually go for – AKA the knob type.

We queued up outside the venue *Gatsby's*, a little vintage, quirky bar nearby to me, for a good hour, and from where I was stood I could see the backstage door.

A guy with golden blonde hair, sharp saintly green eyes and a well-trimmed beard caught my eye. He had a red blazer on contrasting his black jeans and OCD white converse. I got a little flutter inside. I quite liked him, even from that distance.

Good God woman get a grip, I thought, he's probably not even interested in your twenty-six-year-old divorced self who lives in an apartment that doesn't even have an oven.

The rest of the girls in the queue were in their teens dressed up to the nines, stilettos making them all look like replica Karlie Kloss's – I doubted he'd even noticed me standing there.

~

When we finally got into the gig venue, the supporting acts had already started – they weren't so bad.

They had a good beat but were rather shouty for my old self. I mean, there's Rock N Roll Stones style, and then there's Rock N Roll that makes you lose your hearing for a good week.

After about half an hour the lights went down and *The Rainer's* walked on... including the guy I had seen at the back-door entrance.

The guy in the red blazer.

Oh my gosh. He was the lead singer. And he had also added a hat to his already rocking outfit. Talk about a guy who knew what he was doing in every sense.

He came across quite shy from where I was stood, as his fingers nervously played with his tousled hair and his chiseled jawline. Fuck me. Literally. Please do.

The spotlight shone down on him like he was a Greek God made of chocolate and marshmallows and everything you'd ever want to stuff into your mouth...

Oh, my goodness. If it's possible to fall in love with someone without knowing them then I certainly did. After a while, whilst the band played their music and took the whole audience into a euphoria, I yelled into Jodie's heavily pierced ear, "Who's that guy!! The guy in red!?"

"I think it's err...what's his name, err, damn it!"

Jodie paused, thinking, "Oh I know! It's FRED!!!"
Jodie yelled at full volume just as the song faded
into the bridge.

And Fred, the red blazer guy, somehow (god knows
how) heard Jodie's foghorn voice shouting his name
and stared my way.

He looked at me. I mean he *really* looked at me.

Hamilton hadn't looked at me in that way in years,
perhaps even ever. Oh, good god woman. Control
yourself.

For the next two hours of the concert I shook my
stuff and jumped higher than anyone else in the
crowd (benefit of wearing Converse instead of
stilettos).

This sudden urge of youth and flirtatiousness
overcame my usual reserved, sensible, adult self.
Fred had this cute way of dancing, and I got rather
turned on by it. It was like the Horny bug had
infected me with a double dose of horny-take-me-
now-I-ness.

~

As the concert came to an end and the drummer
finished off the set, my heart started beating. Fast.
Like a ticking clock in the final minutes of your
GCSE exam.

I'd never really thought of Fred as a sexy, take me now type of name. But, I tell you what, boy oh boy he could have been called Bernard and I would have jumped on him right there and then.

The crowds started to leave, so Jodie and I made our way to the VIP area. We were greeted by Jodie's acquaintance Natalie, the band manager, who seemed lovely and very, very work orientated. She was one of those people that looked rich with her Gucci earrings and fitted Ralph Lauren skirt and blazer, but she didn't act like she was rich. She was genuine, and overly friendly in a touchy-feely kind of way - and I took to her immediately.

Natalie, or Nat as she encouraged us to call her, said that the boys were just showering and freshening up before coming to the after party. I was kind of bummed about it. There's something exciting about a guy being all sweaty and sticky and... all... manly, but hey, I wasn't going to complain when he came out smelling as fresh as a daisy.

Jodie and I nipped back to the apartment in the meantime to change into something a little more fun, returning in stilettos and boob-pushing dresses. More of the boob-pushing being for me as I am not blessed or gifted in that area.

When we returned, the boys were still getting ready (boys, typical), so we headed over to the bar and

Jodie ordered us some intricate Espresso-Sambuca shot that looked rather appetizing, but really was a let down on the taste buds. Though, it made me feel a little flushed and a little readier to meet this guy I was slowly falling for. My head was spinning...Woah, caffeine high.

Natalie came over and said that the boys would be out any minute, and then asked Jodie if she'd like to go and get a drink and discuss the property sale. Jodie kissed me on the top of my head and said, "Don't be a slut okay darling? Actually, do. You deserve a good bit of nooky, isn't that right Nat? Laters you beautiful little peanut." Then she paused before saying, "Oh, and have you met Fred?" *How I Met Your Mother* style, sneakily walking away as she did.

Gosh she's got a way with words, even to this day.

Out of the corner of my eye I saw a blurred red figure. It was him. I froze. I hadn't properly chatted to a guy in a while and I just went blank. I froze.

Flashbacks of my last date nightmare came into my head as I remembered how I'd sat laughing uncontrollably at the fact he had had a bogey on the edge of his nose, and was as - or possibly even more boring - than a banana. And well, I'd tried the whole Tinder thing but nearly had a mental breakdown when one guy called Rufus super liked me, who looked about seventy-five, and had

Instagram snaps of him and his great grandkids. Yes, GREAT ones. Not just GRAND ones.

My hands were shaking and sweating very unattractively, and I'm pretty sure that my cheeks were crimson (facial ones to those who were thinking I was talking about other cheeks). I looked like a moldy strawberry. I quickly checked my hair in the glossy, mirrored liquor shelf behind the bar and did a quick tongue sweep to check for any unwanted guests staying in Hotel De La Teeth.

Suddenly, scaring me half to death, Red Blazer sat down beside me and whispered, "I hear you already know my name, but what's yours Miss Pink Converse?"

Oh. Shitballs. He *had* spotted me in the queue outside. He had spotted *me* – he must have done because I'd gotten changed since then. Pink Converse were safely in their box in my apartment. I did a quick once over the room to see if anyone else had Converse on, but all I saw were teens in miniskirts and 45-inch wedges. He knew the colour of my shoes.

Oh my, talk about a guy who doesn't miss much.

His tone was so husky and it sounded as if he'd smoked about a thousand cigarettes, but he obviously hadn't because his breath smelt fresh and pure like an angel sent from heaven. And he had a

Southern American drawl, perhaps Arizona way. Dreamy. Oh my god, I nearly dribbled all down my face at the sheer sight of him. Pass the bib.

I looked down shyly then turned to face him taking, the deepest breath I ever have taken.

"Hi...my name's Posy...you were great in the concert..." I babbled, "I mean, you're such a good singer... and the band is so good – I mean, I've never seen you guys before... but I would definitely like to see you again... well not just you but you know, the band and..."

I was babbling still when he said, "Don't worry about telling me your entire life story right now, we've got all night for that honey, and much more if you wish."

I gazed at him. Who was this guy? He spoke in riddles but it made so much sense to me.

I think he liked me, but I couldn't be sure. In a room of six-foot leggy blondes why was he talking to me? That was until he did something very magical. My breathing was still going ten to the dozen like an excitable puppy.

He stood up and placed one of his godly hands onto my bronzed shoulder, my body doing somersaults and backflips.

"Well Miss Posy, I don't want to sound forward but I couldn't take my eyes off you tonight. It seems like you haven't done this in a while and I don't want to make you do anything you don't want to do, but look, here's my number," he said and slid a napkin with a sharpie inscribed digit sentence on it. "And if you feel like a dance tonight or perhaps tomorrow, well let's just say, the answer is always yes. When you're ready."

And with that, he walked away, his feet hitting the floor in time to the sound of Ray Charles' blues oozing from the speakers, leaving me mesmerized.

His spicy, sultry scent lingered around the barstool next to me and I watched him fade away into the darkness of the backstage area. I would have taken a big sniff to try and capture his smell but felt that was just a tad psycho... No, don't go... Don't leave me, I urged in my head...

Oh, what the hell. Downing the last of my espresso-something I grabbed my purse and followed where Red Blazer was going. I forgot the napkin etched with his number in my rush to find him, and left it on the bar.
I lost him in the blur of the after-party buzz, and so had to resort to nosying around to see where he'd gone. He was nowhere to be seen. Shit. Why do we always let the good ones go?

Feeling clammy and hot from the sweaty, rocky

bodies, I pushed the exit door open and headed out into the coolness of the midnight.

Suddenly someone grabbed me and pushed me up hard onto the wall. All at once his lips closed over mine, hard and passionate. He kissed me so desperately, like he needed someone to love him and I kissed him back, pouring myself into the depths of his heavenly, satisfying mouth. His hands were in my hair and our bodies were touching, and this was all new, yet so familiar to me.
This was the type of passion I had been looking for in France, in Ireland and even in Kent. I thought I had found it in Austria, but this was another level. There I was in Barcelona, and finally, *finally* it had happened.

His hips were pushed right into mine, making my back press up against the rough, graphited wall. I felt as sexy as Anastasia when good old Mr. Grey pushes her up against the elevator wall in Fifty Shades.

Unexpectedly Fred pulled away leaving my lips apart in shock, my body craving more touch from this handsome stranger – and I looked down and saw why…

"I am so sorry, this has never happened before, oh my god. Shit. Sorry. I don't mean to come on so strong," He said his hands covering himself.

I chuckled and looked down to see Little Fred trying to make an appearance by bursting out of Big Fred's skinny jeans.

I bent over giggling and it completely brought the atmosphere back to being non-awkward. Both of us were unable to breathe through the laughter, but then we recovered. That was until I said "Look, maybe Little Fred just wanted to say hello... he's only being polite."

And with my fabulous one liner we both collapsed onto the damp concrete floor, tears of laughter streaming down our faces. How two strangers can connect within one evening is the type of magic that still baffles me even to this day. It's the Peter Pan mind-blowing kind of shit.

"Look, let's start this from the beginning again," Fred began with a cheeky grin on his face, "My name's Fred Bayer, named after the great Freddie King and my friends call me Freddie, but I want you to be more than a friend, so I *guess* you could have the special privilege of calling me Frederick like my dear old Mother did."

I laughed. This guy had the cheeky humour every girl wanted. He was handsome too. *And* he dressed all quirky which is one thing I noticed I liked about guys after I left Hamilton.

Hamilton always dressed in a boring plain grey suit.

And no, not Christian Grey *grey*. He was too safe fashion wise, this guy was dangerous, and boy did my libido and I like it.

Chapter 3

FREDDIE

I'm on Fire

I couldn't stop thinking about her; her dark brown eyes and the way she shyly twiddled her hair between her fingers, trying to hide her beautiful blushing cheeks. We had only seen each other the night before, but I couldn't wait any longer to see her and so I forced my manager to ask Jodie to get a hold of Posy's email address or number – some way of getting in touch with her.

Fearless courage was the only thing that made me go up and talk to Posy that night.
I knew she was way out of my league but just looking at her made me lose my mind.

Natalie sent me Posy's number a couple of hours later and as soon as I had her number I went into complete panic.

What should I text her? Did she even like me? Had my little accident made her think I was some kind of sex maniac with erectile priapism?

I was just a guy from a band who wore clothes most guys wouldn't. I wasn't the typical heartbreaker you see in the movies, you know, the Ryan Gosling type.

I had my flaws... one being my solitary crooked bottom tooth. My last girlfriend had mentioned that maybe in the future I should think about getting braces, you know, ready for any future wedding photos – but why change something about yourself that one day might be the reason the *one* falls in love with you?

I had never really fallen for a girl before, mainly because my first ever 'love' – if you can even call it that – ran off with my best friend and is now married with twins, living in a mansion somewhere. I don't feel any hatred for her or any need to go and get revenge by sleeping with all her friends – I'm not that type of guy. And for some reason, it had always been the easier option to put my music first.

I was totally self-conscious as to what to write to Posy, mainly because I had severe dyslexia – the only time my dyslexia doesn't affect me is when I am reading or writing lyrics and sheet music. When I was younger, it was almost as if as soon as I started singing, my entire world of worries turned into a blissful haven of happiness. I always felt as if I was on the outside, until I found music, or until music found me.

~

School hadn't been a pleasant experience – I'd been bullied by mostly everyone, including my so-called friends. I was just this guy that spent his lunchtimes in the music room practicing chords on the guitar and keyboard, or writing down my feelings and making them into jumbled attempts of lyrics.

I'd sometimes even stay behind after school and hide in the toilets in case Billy Johnson was waiting for me at the gates. He was the clever guy in the class, and also the pack leader – he picked on me and my spelling. I got called a wimp, a pussy, a dweeb – all sorts of things. Kids can be real mean.

One day I blew. I hit Billy right back and he never ever hurt me again. It took me six years of unhappiness and zero support from teachers to make that decision. I don't like violence as a rule but Billy was the exception.

~

I had a really happy childhood following my first year of being abandoned by my birth mother. That sounds so deep, but let me explain.

My adoptive mother had taken me under her wing when I was about thirteen months old after she had given up on finding someone to start a family with – ironically the man of her dreams (and the man I now call Dad) turned up a year later!

I don't have any brothers or sisters – though both my Mum and Dad used to be hardcore hippies so I wouldn't be surprised if someone turned up at our door asking for their long-lost parent. But hey, what a story that'd be.

And besides, I would have loved a brother to have been alongside me in school, when I felt my worst – when some days I would cry myself to sleep telling myself that getting angry with the bullies wouldn't get me anywhere. That would have been someone I could talk to without feeling stupid and vulnerable.

The happiness of my childhood abruptly ended when I came home to find my Mum sat shivering on the cold wooden floor.

It was all a blur.

I remember flashing blue lights, my Dad collapsing onto the floor beside me, and my Mum lying on a white bedsheet, lifeless.

She died three days later. The cancer got her. It still

breaks me into pieces if I ever let my mind drift back to that day. The image of my Mum, grey to the bone. It never leaves you. The memories, some good, some bad, stick with you.

High school was a blur after losing my Mum. That time I lost the one Mum I really *had* wanted to keep.

I messed about in high school, I was branded Fidget Bum by Mr. Ainsley – I seemed to try and act that way to distract people from my spelling, my weakness, my inaccuracy.

One teacher, Miss Star (ironically, she was a star, and my first proper teacher crush) kept me behind one day and told me how talented I was.

No other teacher had ever told me that, or even praised me for my very poor effort at trying to spell the big words that got topsy-turvy up in my head. After so many years of bullying and teachers putting me down for not trying hard enough or for being so silly that I couldn't even spell the word silly right – Miss Star came and brightened up my life. She was the Miss Honey of Mesa High. Ironically, she looked just like Posy.

My last years of high school were brightened by my new best friend Josh who also had dyslexia, and had been kicked out of his previous school for being a nuisance.

We managed to build one another up and we imagined this wall around us that meant that no one could ever stop us from reaching for the stars. No longer would a teacher or a silly Billy Johnson stop us from achieving what we had always been told was impossible for people like us.

A year later, Josh and I found a few others alike and made a band.

Six years later, that same high school band, now known as *The Rainer's* were touring Latin America and at one of our headline concerts, there in the front row was no other than Billy 'The Bully' Johnson.

That felt pretty awesome, I must admit.

~

I sat typing out various messages, frustrated at myself for not being able to be as smooth in writing as I had been when I'd spoken to Posy the night before.

I kept reading what I'd written, then I'd lose my place and get frustrated at myself. So, I called Josh because he knew how frustrating the dyslexia was and knew how to boost my confidence. He was also my go to friend when I had a mind blank on lyrics – though with Posy there was never going to be a lyrical mind blank ever again.

Josh guided me through some examples of what he had initially texted his now fiancée and gave me a little advice – in a nutshell, just be yourself and stop worrying about getting your heart broken.

So, taking a deep breath, I constructed a text and didn't even bother to check it for any red squiggly lines – I wanted her to know the real me. I'd never showed anyone *him* before. And by him, I mean the real me… let's not get back onto that embarrassing moment with Little Fred last night. Way to make a first impression Freddie.

After a few paces around the kitchen debating if I should send it, I caught a glimpse of my pathetic self in the mirror and thought what the hell. Clicking send I popped my phone back into my pocket and headed out for a walk.

I wasn't going to sit and stare at my phone like some desperate romantic – even though by definition that's what I've always been.
I take after my Mum and Dad, they loved each other like they've known each other from the very beginning. The way they looked at each other, that's how I feel about Posy, and the way they laughed with one another – it's rare to see these days.

Chapter 4

POSY

Horny Hornerton

Fred and I met up a day later following the concert, and can I just say that one day felt like FOREVER. Every song that came on the radio reminded me of him in some way. He was like some crazy dream that I guess I'd never thought would become my reality.

He had asked Natalie, his manager, to ask Jodie for my number because he was too impatient waiting for me to contact him - so I'd been informed. And so, the morning after the night where Little Fred made an appearance I received a text from his truly...

Hello stranger, remember me?

Hoping to see you sometime today. Make sure to wear your pink converse if you accept my offer, and I'll wear mine to match. Just kidding. Pink's not my colour, I'm more of a fuchsia kind of guy – did I spell fuchsia, right? ;)

I promise if you accept, Little Fred won't make an appearance this time.
I hope you've been thinking about me as much as I have you.

Yours,
Freddie X

Oh my gosh. I reread the text repeatedly, pinching myself and wondering where this guy had been my entire life. He was like a modern-day Mr. Darcy, with a mobile phone and he was *even* sexier. He had this magical way with words that just made my entire body urge just to hear his voice, amongst other urges which I hoped would be coming very soon, in the non-sluttiest kind of way.

I thought about his eyes the most. It was like they knew me - he saw parts of me that nobody ever had even flicked an eyelid at.

He looked at me like a musician looking at their piano, taking in all 88 keys – except he didn't just see me in black and white, he saw me in polaroid colour.

I remembered that I'd told Jodie we would go down to the harbor in the evening, but when I showed her the text from Freddie she first of all screamed for about ten minutes straight and then exclaimed, "Oh my gosh, GO! GO have a drink with him, and then if all goes well bring him home and have rampant sex darling! After all, he's got a cute butt."

I wasn't sure about the rampant sex part but I sure as hell wanted to kiss him again… and again. He was so good at kissing. He was the perfect equilibrium between guys who seem to be that hungry that you nearly lose your tongue, or the ones that literally leave you with a wet chin from their escapable and excitable puppy-like slobber. So that was a tick on my list.

So, after confirming my cancellation with Jodie, I didn't hesitate a second longer in texting him back…

Hello Red Blazer,

Funnily enough I do remember you, and yes, you've been on my mind too.

See you tonight at Gatsby's? I'll be there at 8:30 and promise not to be too fashionably late.

Posy x

P.s. Don't leave Little Fred home, he might get lonely...

And I hit send and blushed at my p.s. note. I felt like a teenager being all flirty and flushed.

~

My shift waitressing could not go by quick enough – though all of the staff wanted to know who this mystery fella was, I just wanted to see *him* again. I wanted to stop talking to everyone else about him, and actually go and talk *to* him, maybe even kiss those soft, baby-bum textured lips once again... Oh my.

My last customer had the biggest order you could imagine possible – it consisted of that many food allergy notes and queries over the cleanliness of the restaurant I very nearly threw my little crappy waitress pen at his hairy face. But I resisted in case I got arrested for harassing a customer and ended up in a Spanish jail, and consequently missed out on my date with Freddie.

As soon as the clock struck 8pm (sounding a little Cinderella-esque I know) I dashed across the Square and along the cobbled street, scrambled up to my apartment and quickly got ready.

Women have so much to choose from – it's not just

a case of getting dressed.

For example, take underwear – the question is, is there any chance there could be any sexy sex tonight? Well, if so I better pop on my red lacey knickers and push up bra. Or do I not opt for the push up bra because that's then giving him a false illusion that I have huge, voluptuous breasts when in actual fact they are the tiniest tits ever crafted. Then you've got to consider if wearing that type of underwear on the second date is just making you look like a slut who's too easy with men, so then there comes the debate of, "Fine, I guess I'll just opt for my granny period knickers and act like I'm a Nun, when in actual fact what I really want to do doesn't even involve knickers."

In the end, I stuck to the red underwear that I had first chosen, threw on a mini black skirt and a heart patterned pink blouse, finishing the outfit off with my pink Converse, as requested. Then I quickly slathered on some gloss, a touch of mascara which very nearly caused me to go blind after poking myself in the eye with the wand thingamajig, and dashed out of the door. I took a quick look at my watch as I locked the door and it was 8:32pm. Fashionably late indeed...

~

As I headed along the aesthetically pleasing streets lined with the locals and splendid Spanish serenades, I realized how much I had come to love Barcelona.

I rounded the corner and I saw him from the blurred edge of my eye, but pretended I hadn't clocked him to avoid the awkward, "Do I wave or not?" dilemma when you're too near for a wave, but you feel you need to do *something*. Ah – you know what I mean.

He was wearing a Bruce Springsteen T-Shirt with a denim waistcoat, black cropped jeans and those OCD, white Converse. From where I was stood I could see his heart was beating as fast as mine, his eyes focused on only me, and mine only on him.

As I got closer, I did something that I know to this day he will never forget. I went and tripped over. But the thing is, I didn't even trip over a cobble, or just have a little wobble - oooohhh poet and I didn't know it. Yup - I actually tripped over my own foot, face planted the floor, with my knickers on full view and screamed, "Oh Fuck!" in front all of the guests eating beautiful, elegant delicacies outside Gatsby's.

Freddie dashed over to me, and I could see he had a cheeky smirk on his face.

I managed to get myself into a sitting position and cross my legs like you used to have to do in shitty school assemblies.

Oh god, I used to get such bad cramp in my arse cheeks in those boring things.

Jodie had actually got 'dead arse' so bad once that she went to stand up to collect an award (yep a rare occasion where Jodie got an award) but her legs forgot to work, and she face planted the floor and landed on top of the extremely pissed off Math teacher behind us.

I looked up at Freddie (and by the way, it's rather a good view from a sitting position) and he hoarsely said, "Well, you certainly know how to make an entrance, don't you darling?"

All of a sudden, his face turned into sheer concern, "Oh my god, your knee – it's bleeding." He shouted something in Spanish to one of the waiters, and they came running back with a damp cloth and a bandage.

First and foremost, he spoke Spanish. Second, he SPOKE FRICKIN' SPANISH. Oh MY god, I remember thinking, *take me now*. Right there, on the cobbles. I don't mind a few lumps and bumps beneath me. Don't judge ladies (and gentleman) - if you'd have been there, the exact same fantasy would have been going through your head too. Don't even try and deny it.

I was abruptly distracted from my fantasy when Fred dabbed the icy cloth on my knee and I nearly

yelped "Fuck that's cold!" but switched it to a very
reserved and conservative, "Ouchy!"

"What am I going to do with you Mrs?" he
whispered as he took a seat beside me on the
cobbles, his hand still gently resting the ice on my
grazed kneecap.

I giggled, "Well, I've got some ideas." And I winked.
Oh my god. I remembered thinking how naughty I
was and wondering *what* has gotten into me... or
more like, what hasn't gotten *in* to me. Sigh.
He laughed out loud and his eyes lit up as he
caressed my satisfied ambiance.

He took my hand and smoothed his fingers over it,
capturing my full attention. Gotta love a man who
has nice hands.

"Do you want me to kiss it better?" he murmured in
a soft, sexy voice.

I smiled flirtatiously and said, "You know you
shouldn't take advantage of an injured woman. And
besides, we wouldn't want Little Fred to make
another appearance, now would we?"

Then, without hesitation and ever so naturally I
kissed him softly, and lingered on his lips for a
while, slowing feeling the interchange of passion
and sexual tension between us. He was a
wonderland and I was tumbling down, head over

heels, forgetting reality.

My crazy dream.

Chapter 5

POSY

Je Ne Sais Quois

Barcelona was my last travelling venture, but many months before that I had begun my travels cautiously, when I left my hometown of Kent and I headed for France. I know, not quite the je nais se quois of travelling destinations, but it gave me that opportunity of dipping my toe in the water.

When in France, I took a house-sitting job, unbeknown to me the job was in a household run by an absolute nut-job named Theo.

I remember sitting in my bed, mummified by my elephant-decorated duvet in my dingy, little flat in Kent and searching for cheap ways to travel.

A House-Sitting website popped up. In my mind, I was imagining I'd housesit somewhere and meet Jude Law like Cameron Diaz did in *The Holiday*, but there's such a thing known as shit luck! Which I seem to have become best friends with in the past.

I went for the place closest to home, but not too far just to make the distance of moving a little easier – France it was.

I came across a quaint little farmhouse on the House-Sitting website, it looked so Snow White-esque, so friendly. It turned out to be the complete opposite.

I arrived at what can only be described as a shack. The house I had seen on the website was the *owner's* house – the shed in the garden was *all mine*. Oh, wasn't I a lucky girl. To add to my suffering, the house owner, Theo, was such a pain in the arse.

The ad had read: 'looking for a helper for around the house, just 2 hours of light duties each day.'

Light duties my arse.

I am not exaggerating here; firstly, while in France, I was woken up by Theo's morning 'shouting yoga' session out on the terrace which pissed me right off.

THEN I had a second wakeup call from this bloody rooster, or whatever the hell it was in the barn next to me. I swear that thing was out to get me.

The food wasn't so bad; breakfast was essentially an overdose of croissants. Lunch, a French baguette, and dinner was usually anything attributed to the French culture accompanied with lots of red wine to drown out Theo's blabber, and help me to sleep through his shouting yoga sesh each morning.

Then Theo would constantly badger me to do various jobs – and they weren't jobs you'd have volunteers queuing up for, shall we say.

One highly memorable job was cleaning the pigs using the garden hose. Firstly, pigs freak the hell out of me, and second they smell… like shit. I'm vegetarian myself which should mean that I should love every animal and I do, but those pigs were just eyeing me right up. I think the writer of 'Babe' was looking at a different type of pig when he was writing. 'Babe' was cute; these things would stare me down. You don't get many people asking, "Hey, are you a pig person?" now do you?

So, on the first (and last) try of the pig-cleaning job, I turned the bloody hose on by accidentally leaning my big bum on the switch so that the water squirted at my face.

Then I eventually got the hose the right way, sprayed it at the pig, which then started chasing me. It chased me out of the barn and onto the country road... so I ran and ran and never went back to Theo's again.

I spent the remaining month working in a café, so that I could scrape by and afford a place at the Inn. I felt like the Virgin Mary. Except there was no Joseph to go along with my room in the Inn. And definitely no chance of a conception with my dodgy uterus and lack of activity in the sexual playing field.

I spent a total of two weeks at Theo's, which I think I deserve a medal for. I mean, I literally got chased away. By pigs.

As I said, I worked at a café for that remaining month, it was called 'Café Formidable', and that was where I fell in love with a memorable customer.

He would come in every Friday evening, becoming a regular of mine and I instantly liked him.
He had these dark, erotic eyes, and he would just intensely stare at me. It was as if time had stopped, and his whole world was this scruffy, blonde chick in front of him.

I remember ringing my brother, Noah, numerous times, drooling on about how this hot French guy who could visit my Eiffel Tower at any time.

Noah and I had built our relationship on a dirty sense of humour and love, and god knows what I would do without him. He always encourages me to do what will make me happy, not many people out there take the time to remind you that sometimes you have to think about yourself.

Whilst on the phone to him one day, I could hear Jessie and Niall going nuts in the background (must take after their Aunty Posy – ha!) and I asked where Iz was.

"Oh, she's working overtime," Noah replied quietly.

"Again?" I asked, with a concerned tone, thinking about how my beautiful niece and nephew must miss their Mum. She was just never home. A workaholic some might say, but it had reached a point where I had to say something. She was *always* working overtime and quite frankly it got on my (tiny) tits.

"Noah – does she really have to work all this over time? Why isn't she home? It's a Sunday evening, she should be with her family. You've got to do something about this – it's not fair on the kids."

The line went quiet for a while and Noah simply said, "I've asked her and she said she can't argue with her boss."

I took a deep, anger-filled breath and answered, "It's

just not good enough, and I know it isn't any of my business but you know I worry about you and those lovely little'uns. Just let me know if you ever need me. Call anytime okay? I've got to go… okay? See you soon Noah."

~

Every Thursday evening, I would make an effort to shave my legs, just in case my French fantasy would come to life. And one Friday, it did. Quick question - is there really a secret way of shaving your legs in the shower without falling on your arse or getting your leg stuck in midair? If there is you guys have got to tell me. ASAP.

So, on this Friday night, I was walking out of the back door of the cafe, after locking up. It was around midnight, and I heard a car engine running.

It was him.

He waved shyly, and stepped out of his car.
He walked up to me, and kissed me. Hard. His breath smelt like coffee beans and was warm on my neck. I hadn't felt this close to someone in so long. I didn't want to stop. And so, it happened. In the car and kind of on it too. I know. Don't judge. Girls have needs. And, besides, I wasn't turning down a hot Frenchman on a lonely Friday evening.

After he dropped me home, I walked up to my

apartment, my head spinning. I tripped up one of the steps because I wasn't watching where I was going, and I heard a disapproving shout from elsewhere in the corridor over my clumsiness. I literally danced into my apartment, feeling like a diamond, so treasured, so valued by someone. I felt special.

But all wasn't as it seemed. The next morning, Café Formidable was awfully busy. A typical Saturday morning. I was rushed off my feet and got into a heated argument with this heavily pregnant woman, accompanied by two screaming babies, who claimed she needed a table for four, and that her husband would be there any second. Bearing in mind I was ordered by my boss to only give out tables to customers in concrete forms, not the imaginary "Oh they will be here any minute" customers.

After a lot of persuasion, I put the angered lady on a table because frankly I was still feeling all euphoric from the night before, and could not be bothered in attempting to argue back. As I was serving another customer, the woman I had argued with shouted me over, pointed to the window and said with her French accent, "You, you, err Waitress, see, see, I told you my 'usband was coming."

And there he was.

My French fantasy was in fact a married Dad of two, with another on the way, who had fooled me every Friday evening by taking off his wedding ring.

I didn't really know how to react. I was numb, and even more hurt by the fact that *he* pretended to have never seen me before, or been to the café. He claimed that's why he was late meeting his wife – he couldn't find 'Café Formidable'. He had a good dose of spit in his food from me and a dash of outdated eggs to give him a good dose of the shits (I had informed the chefs about my situation). Women can be brutal you know, so don't act like a shit otherwise we'll find a way of giving you the shits, okay?

That day, I kept thinking, why do I always attract knobs? And no. Not in a good way. The type of knobs you don't want in your life.

But something changed inside me that day. I'd had enough of Hamilton's, and French guys. I whipped off my apron, and walked out of that place a new woman. I rented a bike from the tourist center and rode around Lille all day. The sun shone down, warming my golden cheekbones and lightening my spirits. The wind blew my hair gently, making it tickle my shoulder blades and whisper in my ears.

Placing my foot down on the ground, I came to a holt at the edge of the Cathedral. Its tall grey exterior stood high above me, unreachable. I'm not religious in anyway but I believe in there being something, I don't know how to explain it – I just guess I hope that when this life ends, it doesn't just end there, you know?

As the sun started to set in Lille, I returned my bike and made my way back to my apartment, pausing along Bahada Road to grab a well-deserved Crêpe, drowned in lemon and sprinkled with sugar.

As I walked, I enjoyed every sensation around me, the warm taste of the Crêpe, the feel of the cool sunset, the noise of the sleepy town. Everything enticed me. France had become my home, but I was ready to say goodbye, and so I took one last glance, one last touch of everything around me, and decided to catch a flight home the next day.

When I got back to the Inn that evening I switched into my slouchy clothes, scraped my hair up into a low ponytail and flicked on the radio. As the music filled the room, I walked out onto the balcony and twirled around, my bare feet reminding me of my aliveness on the cold, uneven tiles beneath me.

My dancing was interrupted by a knock at the door. Walking over to the radio beside my bed, I turned the volume down, and hesitantly made my way to the door. It was approaching 11pm – who could need me at this time?

I peered through the peep hole and saw someone who made my heart flutter for all the wrong reasons. It was him, 'Café Formidable' guy.

Taking a deep breath, I had a think about what to do, how to respond. I could open the door and continue my love affair, or I could be the very intelligent and skillful twenty-six-year-old that I am *occasionally* able to be. Emphasis on the occasionally there.

He knocked again, this time pretty impatiently. I stripped down, whipping off my bra and threw that over one chair, my knickers across the sofa. I wanted it to look authentic. Let the plan commence…

I grabbed my bed sheet and wrapped it around me. Then, very nearly bursting out laughing at the thought of my evil plan, I approached the door and started banging myself up against it making various sounds and shouting "Oh, yes, right there, don't stop!" and "Oh Baby, you're the best I've ever had!". I wanted to remind the French guy what a shit he had been. And besides, insult a man's penis and boy have you won.

Then, after my final fake climax sound I peered through the hole in the door. He was still there. Dirty pervert.

So, my revenge and sensational acting continued, talking to the imaginary guy that I'd just had sex with I shouted, "Hey, I think there's someone at the door, I'll go and get rid of them!"

I then approached the door, dropping my bed sheet a little to give this guy a glimpse of what he would never be touching ever again and opened the latch slightly.

He looked at me, and said, "Look Posy, I realize this is a très bad time, but I don't want you giving up on what we could be, chéri."

I actually laughed out loud.

After a deep, annoyed sigh I replied, "Look you... you... you... fuckwank! *I* am busy right now if you haven't already heard, and according to my knowledge, *you* should be *busy* with your wife and kids right now. I'm not that type of girl, and never would be if you would have been honest with me. Either leave now, or I'll call the guy I've just been having the best sex I've ever had with because he's a policeman and he can escort you home. What do you think of that... Dickprick?"

And just to emphasize my power and sassiness I finished the sentence off with a much-awaited door slam.

Yeah, he left. And I never saw him again. And I felt awesome. Hashtag girl power. Oscar nomination for Posy? I think so.

I spent the rest of the evening dancing around the apartment to Dire Straits until my feet hurt. And then collapsed onto the sofa and managed to find enough Wi-Fi to catch an episode of *Made in Chelsea*. Sad, I know, but I felt empowered by my performance. Plus, who doesn't want to ogle Sam Thompson and Jamie Laing on *Made in Chelsea*? Can't resist a posh boy. Also, *MIC* reminded me that it wasn't just me dealing with relationship problems and cheating partners. Reality TV can be really good for the heart sometimes, though Mum has no other opinion than it being 'utter shite'.

Chapter 6

POSY

When We Were Young

My ex-husband, Hamilton had been my first crush. We had been in each other's Art class and he was a known player, but *he* chased *me*, which was a new, unexpected move in his game at the time.

In high school, I wasn't particularly the known hottie – I mean, I was the girl who pranced around wearing dungarees with holes in the knees, and a polka-dot bandana wrapping my blonde curls up. I certainly wasn't the hottest dish on the high school menu.

The hot dish was actually Cressida Jeems (AKA Queen Bitch), the 6ft Model type with a wafer-thin stomach and Snow-White skin.

Cressida Jeems was my 'best friend' at the time. Note the air quotes there.

High School was just a blur of a reenactment of Mean Girls, minus the sweet, gentle Aaron Samuels.

There was certainly a fair share of Regina George's, and up until Hamilton had won me over, those Regina's had waited for me outside the school gates after school and bullied me for years. Probably one stupid reason why I stayed with Hamilton. He kept me safe. He changed my past. He made me feel higher than I had done before.

Hamilton was the type of guy who every girl loved, adored and would have quite frankly dropped their drawers for in an instant. He was the cool DJ at the Friday night roller skating disco that our whole year group went to each week.

I'm still not sure why he picked me to chase after – like I said, I wasn't anything special. There were blond stick insects at his feet and Victoria Beckham's a plenty, but he wouldn't leave me alone.

He would skate up behind me after his jamming session had finished and hold onto me, trying desperately to talk to me in every possible way he could. It was the oddest thing in the whole wide world, but he protected me when people commented on how I dressed, and remarked on how dressing unique was the reason why he had fallen for me.

Ironically, after that rumour went around, about a hundred girls invested in a pair of dungarees.

~

There was only one other guy prior to Hamilton and he was a *lot* older than me. He was a paramedic that I'd happened to cross paths with after Jodie drank a little *too* much *red red wiiiiiine* and walked into a lamppost, knocking herself unconscious and breaking her nose in three places.

She was always the wilder one out of the two. When she broke her nose, she had to go to the hospital and to be honest we did have a blast in the hospital, especially when I got to wheel her around the halls at 100mph. Cheap thrills. And there's a story to go along with this, so let me take you through the events of the nose-breaking evening. After Jodie's lamppost run in, panicking that she was dead or something, I rang 999 and the ambulance came screeching around the corner, blue lights flashing and the sirens making a piercing noise in the quietness of the night.

That's when I met the first and only guy I would ever sleep with prior to Hamilton and his name was Cody.

He turned out to be an absolute dick *but* it's a story worth telling - you'll see why.

He approached me in his green overalls and black worker boots, I had little flutters in my stomach. There was something in the air, something quite magical passing between us. He had efficiently packed Jodie up, with his colleague, onto the stretcher and placed her inside the ambulance, telling me constantly that she would be alright – the worry on my face was far from unnoticeable. The amount of blood on Jodie's face was discomforting, but he said that she was in good hands. Hmm, good hands, I thought: *I know what I'd like to do with those hands...*

On the ambulance journey to the nearest hospital he noticed I was shivering and passed me his jacket that he had come to work in. It was a duffel coat type and smelt of *Hugo Boss.* I thanked him shyly, glad of his gentlemanly gesture which prevented my nippy nipples from cutting through my top like two pinpricks.

He looked visibly older than me, and one thing that gave it away was how low his voice was.
Most sixteen-year-olds at my age were still talking as if they'd got something caught in their throat.
We hit it off straight away and chatted throughout the whole journey, he told me about his family, how he had become a paramedic like his Dad, and that he had a younger brother who was going through

his teenage stage. We got through a lot of detail in little time, and you can't do that with many guys. Sure, you can talk to them and flirt, but having a truly meaningful conversation – that's rare.

He was confident too, which unfortunately over time turned into cockiness, in more ways than one. But hey, this is just the beginning of the story.

Cody the paramedic had finished his shift at 1am, but stayed and grabbed a coffee with me in the waiting room, whilst Jodie had surgery on her newly crooked nose.

I was sat next to him in my strapless t-shirt of a dress, with heels that tied all the way up to my knees. I had a sweaty forehead from all the stress of looking after a friend who had nearly killed herself, and chipped black nail varnish from my nervous wait for the ambulance.

He, on the other hand was an image of perfection. He had a really strong Manchester accent, and sounded rather like Gary Barlow, and I totally have the hots for that type of Northern manliness. Don't ask.

He was so well groomed, his hair literally trimmed to inches of precision and hair sprayed with military precision. Oh, and he had those types of eyelashes that most girls would die for, or at least spend hours trying to achieve with a crappy volumizing mascara that they've been conned into, without reading the small print.

Jodie ended up having to stay overnight due to the anaesthetic and I was told to come and pick her up the next morning. Cody offered to drive me home (benefit of dating an older guy is that you don't have to buy seven train tickets to get home), and rebelliously ignoring the stranger danger message we were preached at in school, I accepted. He drove a huge, black Chevy with luxury interior – and he let me ride shotgun. In the car, I mean. Don't be so dirty minded...

He popped on the radio and we set off home in the darkness. We chatted endlessly and just as I was getting out of his truck, he asked if he could see me again soon.

He added he was kind of glad I'd called 999, and he didn't often say that. We exchanged numbers and I walked back into the house, giddy as if I'd drank a keg of homemade cider.

We saw each other a couple of days later – he took me out to dinner (yes, to dinner like an actual man not to go and *hang* in the park with some *mates*). He wore a white crisp shirt tucked into jeans, finishing his outfit with a brown belt.

I had spent hours with Jodie picking out the perfect outfit for myself, though I couldn't understand much of her speech with her nose bandage wrapping around her entire head like she was one quarter mummified. We decided on a little flowery, flowy dress with my little yellow glitter boots, a good dose of jewellery and expensive perfume – I also pinched my Mum's *Chanel* that she always hid right at the top of the en suite cabinet.

The meal was lovely and he passed my usual tests, a) did not eat with his mouth open and/or talk whilst eating, b) did not make sex noises whilst eating and c) did not dribble whilst eating. Trust me, I'd had many dates before him with many guys and they all did either one or all of those.

Oh, and he also passed my politeness test in that he offered to pay – I am a huge believer in feminism but it's still nice to know that someone cares about you and actually wants to treat you. I of course offered to pay half and he declined, and so I promised to treat him the next time we went out.

Again, I once went on a date (one date may I just clarify) with a guy that went into *my* bag and got *my* purse out to pay. I mean, who the hell even does that? Too many fuckwits about these days.

So, Cody and I were dating for a good six months before he made the big move. I remember it was my seventeenth birthday and he booked for us to go away for the night, which in my mind was code for a big milestone.

I was a virgin and had never even had a serious boyfriend my own age, never mind someone ten years older who had obviously had much more experience in that type of trade.

He'd told me that he'd had a long-term girlfriend before me called Mandi, but they had broken it off after she had decided her work was more important, and that she wanted to get more serious than he did.

I felt I had a lot to compete with and so asked Jodie (my slutty best friend) for advice – she won't mind me using that adjective to describe her, she loves her rompy pompy. First Jodie drew me some very intricate diagrams and then she took me shopping and encouraged me to buy some sexy lingerie – quite frankly I bought a piece of string for £60.
I mean, if we're talking price wise, big knickers are cheaper and you get *more* material – and they're comfy.
Thongs scrunch up your arse cheeks that often that you end up walking like you've accidentally sat down on a plug.

A week after my birthday, Cody and I drove down to a little B&B in Brighton and spent our first night together, in the same bed. He had booked it all and it was so romantic and refreshing. I had made the first move after he'd come out of the shower, and was wearing just a towel. We had kissed for a while and it all came so naturally to me – I did everything

Jodie had told me to do and followed all the movements Jodie's diagrams had described.

But there was something very odd, and I nearly (emphasis on the nearly) got the giggles. His thingamajig was a little floppier than I'd expected – he didn't seem to show any excitement towards *you know,* and I had done all the things that needed to be done so that it shouldn't be floppy at all...

He apologized looking at my confused face and said that this was his first time too. I nearly choked in shock. Here was this totally hot guy who was twenty-six-years-old who hadn't yet had sex. And I thought I was old losing my virginity.

"But you said that you and Mandi were together for so long?" I said, confused with his past.

"Yeah, Mandi broke up with me after a year because I wouldn't sleep with her. I just wanted to wait for the right person you know, not waste myself on someone that doesn't really love me for who I am. And, I think you're the right person for me."

I smiled sympathetically and felt a little more relaxed knowing we were both sailing the beginner boat. After a little more encouragement, we had sex for the first time for both of us and it wasn't brilliant I'll admit. It was a little uncomfortable, but everything went where it should and Floppy got its act together eventually.

~

After a glorious nine months of dating Cody, it ended abruptly when he stopped calling and ignored me in the streets, passing me by as if he'd suddenly developed short term amnesia.

I was rather confused to be honest... there was no reason for him to act that way, we'd been doing fine. I mean the bedroom part was a bit bland thanks to Mr. Occasionally Floppy, but we enjoyed seeing each other and didn't even argue.

One night Jodie sat down with me and we discussed all of the options as to why he had suddenly dropped off the radar.
I told her about the sporadic bedroom disaster but she insisted that it happens to them all at some point, and I mentioned that he was a tad bit cocky at times, and that lots of girls looked at him - ones that dressed in proper clothes and not dungarees. But we couldn't quite put our finger on it.

Then Jodie burst out with, "Maybe he's gay?" And I nearly spat my beer out, projectile style.

"No, he can't be gay, I mean, he can't surely be gay... he asked *me* out. *And* he dated a girl before me." I had replied, suddenly trying to weigh up all the factors.

"Well, there's only really one way to find out." Jodie

had exclaimed, grabbing the keys for the door. As we had both had a few beers, Jodie gave me a ride on the back of her BMX (oh the good old days) and we headed for Cody's place.

Bursting in through the door which was luckily open I walked into see a sight I cannot unsee, even to this day.

He *was* in fact gay and that was proven by him fervently humping my fucking high school gym teacher, Mr. Dorsey.

"Oh. Sweet... Caroline." I murmured in utter disbelief, observing the fact that I had lost my virginity to a guy who was actually into guys.

And that, my friends, was the unforeseen end of that.

A few months later, Hamilton had walked into my life and replenished my tarnished reputation that I had lost my virginity to a guy who was now gay.

I had tried for months after to continue a friendship with Cody because we had gotten on so well, but he blatantly ignored me in every respect, and quite frankly he was in the wrong for cheating on me with my gym teacher.

God, life's complicated.

Both Cody and his new BF Mr. Dorsey had seen me in my knickers or gym knickers at some point in life. Oh, what a sight.

Now I'm just picturing myself in those unflattering, pleated netball skirts I used to have to wear for hockey. Why is it that uniform stylists seem to want you to remain a nun for the rest of your entire life?

~

I met Hamilton in my last year of college and we even decided to both go to the same university because we felt we were the *real* thing. I studied an English Major and Hamilton studied his Masters in Law.

I'm pretty sure he's got a PHD now – short for Pathetic Heartless Dick. Ha. I just came up with that on the spot.

Back to my story – so Hamilton and I had started dating when we were seventeen.

Within a few months he had cheated on me with Cressida Jeems. Yes, the Cressida Jeems, the supposed best friend of mine. Though he'd insisted it was only *oral* so it wasn't really cheating.

Considering he was a lawyer in training he certainly needed to check the law on cheating to know that fucking oral is counted in that definition.

So, I'd broken up with him, telling him that I couldn't go out with someone that I couldn't trust.

But he wouldn't stop trying to win me over, and despite my family insisting he was bad news, I went back to him.

It's a very odd feeling being drawn back to something that you know you shouldn't want to get close to. But I was controlled by his force, by his sheer persuasion that he wouldn't ever hurt me again. The heart wants what the heart wants as they say, (I don't know who *they* are though).

And so, after two more years of dating and two long years of studying for our degrees, one late night he got down on one knee… and tied his shoelace. I'm not even kidding. I thought he was going to propose.

Fast forward a few months and he *finally* did. He took me to Manchester and proposed at the Christmas markets, surrounded by a million glistening, ruby lights.

Inside the little black velvet box Hamilton was holding was a Platinum Ritani Diamond Ring. It was so beautiful, but totally not me.

I'm not really sure why he'd chosen it – I'd always pointed out vintage, small designs in the windows of pawn shops, hoping to make his future job a little easier.

The ring was as heavy as Santa's sack as he leaves the North Pole, and was frankly some Kate Middleton type of shit. I was more along the lines of a Drew Barrymore gal who wouldn't complain about a sterling silver ring from Argos. But I loved him, and I took the ring as a symbol of his attempt to try and buy me something to make me feel special.
A year later we married at this huge castle which Hamilton's parents chose; I had wanted something small-scale, just a few friends and family, but it turned out that Hamilton had lots of friends and family.

More than me, that is. Apparently, the 'volume' of guests required a fortress according to Judith, Hamilton's bitch of a Mother.

Jodie had been my only bridesmaid and I had suggested that Noah be the best man, but Hamilton had gotten into a big argument with me about how *I* wasn't supposed to choose the best man. And so, my brother ended up standing right at the back of the chapel as Bitch Judith had given priority front row seats to her family and friends, like she was some yellow-fleece-jacketed attendant at the M.E.N arena. I'm just picturing Bitch Judith in yellow right now actually, and boy would she make an unflattering fucking canary.

We began married life by honeymooning in Barbados in a 5* resort – again my choice had been heading to India to explore the culture and perhaps visit the hidden gems in the mountain tops, but again, Bitch Judith was the clicker of the enter button.

Hamilton had known that I couldn't have children and was okay with it, as he said that he didn't want children anyway. But somewhere deep inside me I did want *something* in the future, and I always kept my hopes up because you hear of so many men changing their minds over time. Hamilton never did. And he didn't open up to my idea of adoption either.

Bitch Judith had always commented on how if I adopted an Asian Child the neighbors might think that I'd had an affair with an Asian man.
Good God Judith, keep up with the times dear and maybe cut down on the racism. Besides, it wouldn't count as an affair if I just had oral with an Asian guy, right Hamilton?

But Hamilton being the Mummy's boy he was listened and went along with everything Judith said. I came second opinion wise – no, wait, third – Hamilton always put himself second. Selfish as a toddler with candy.

It only took me seven, long fucking years to realize that.

Chapter 7

POSY

The Great Gatsby

After recovering from my embarrassing face plant, Fred and I spent the evening talking for hours and hours in a hush-quiet corner of Gatsby's.

We shared a small bowl of Spanish, savory popcorn and every time our hands clumsily met in the bowl there was this electrical current, and boy did it feel good, and yes, I could not stop myself falling, and falling... but thankfully not in the literal sense following my unforgettable entrance.

We talked and talked about life, about how we'd just come across one another – two people from different countries, meeting in a country foreign to them both. Pure magic, and a pure work of fate.

I found that I didn't really want to talk about my past, because I was so happy right there and then, and bringing up unhappy memories would have just dulled a brightly lit, starry sky.

But then something happened that gave me no other choice than to open up and root through my painful memories of what felt like another life.

Gatsby's had a popular jukebox, and whilst I nipped to the toilet (for a number one, I had done many nervous number two's beforehand) Fred went over to choose a song.

As I was exiting the loos - after a quick check in the mirror for any toilet paper on feet or skirt tucked into my sexy red knickers – I heard it.

It wasn't a song that held memories I wanted to relive.

"*She's the One*" by Robbie Williams played throughout the restaurant – it had been our wedding song. It brought back memories of what could have been and I suddenly felt rather pathetically teary. Walking over to our little corner table, Fred was beaming but suddenly his face turned into confusion as I sat down at the table, trying to hide my watery, mascara smudged eyes. He quickly scooted around onto my side of the booth, concerned, "Honey, are you okay? What is it?" he whispered, whilst catching the tears with his fingertips.

I took a deep breath and sighed, "I didn't want to ruin what was such a lovely night but... I was married – his name was Hamilton," I looked up at his face, waiting for a sense of disappointment, but he simply carried on sweetly rubbing the base of my back.

"This used to be our song."

Fred's eyes looked deep into mine, a connection you couldn't even describe in words.

"He cheated on me, numerous times," I continued, "We'd been together since we were teens – looking back now I don't know what I saw in him..." I carried on explaining my life story in a nutshell as our waiter, Andy interrupted us with the arrival of our sharing platter. The poor guy - Andy was used to customers being upbeat when he brought the food over, but Fred's eyes were transfixed on me, and I simply said a brief thank you as Andy walked away.

Andy, who had become a good friend of mine, constantly attempting to set me up with customers and providing me with discounted food, suddenly did a U-Turn, and came back to our booth.

"Look Señorita, I don't mean to interfere here but I've been watching you two all night, and there's something quite, ahh they call it hermosa, about you two. If you've upset her," he said turning to Fred, "Just make it work."

"No, no it's not him," I said, suddenly aware of how our situation must have looked from a distance, "He's lovely. He's more than lovely. It's just problems of the past, ya know?"

Andy smiled wisely and simply spoke, "We Spanish don't live in the past my dear, if we did, I wouldn't be as happy as I am today, in the *presente.*"

And with his wise words Andy moved along to his next customers and as I looked back towards Fred, he too had disappeared.

Oh my gosh. Had I freaked him out? Did it bother him that I had been married? Oh god, maybe my blubbering state had made him think that I still liked Hamilton... Err, no no no. Never in a million years.

I WAS GOING TO BE SINGLE AND ALONE FOREVER...

Then, to my surprise, the bass of "She's the One" began again and someone grabbed my hand – it was Freddie.

"C'mon you, let's make this song ours instead, alright?"

And so there we were, our bodies swaying amongst the fellow couples, some old, some so young that they hadn't yet lived through heartbreak.

We danced for hours, our hands and eyes glued

together, and we kissed tenderly as the darkness and smokiness of Gatsby's made us feel alone in the world, two people becoming one. I kept treading on Fred's toes and we were both so ungraceful it was beyond hilarious.

As Andy, the wisest man in the restaurant, shouted out to the guests that they would be closing soon, Freddie and I were brought back to the real world.

Even though the music stopped, Fred kept hold of me, keeping me close in his arms, his hands resting on the verge of my knicker line, his fingers rubbing small circles along the base of my spine.

As all of the tipsy, full-bellied Spaniards vacated Gatsby's, we did too. Hand in hand we walked along the crisscross paved streets, not uttering a word but knowing exactly what one another was thinking.

We had created something very special and we both knew it.

It had all happened so soon, yet it felt like a lifetime's crafting of forever.

He kept rubbing his thumb across mine in slow, teasing rhythms; a friend of mine had once told me about how hands speak a language of their own, especially the language of love.

I think many couples take for granted the magic feeling of holding someone's hand. Sure, sex is great (as long as it's not with Hamilton), but hand holding is something a little undervalued in my eyes.

We stopped at the square where East lead to his hotel and West to mine. He stroked his thumb across my bottom lip, whilst pulling me towards him, his other hand on the back of my neck.

We kissed. I don't know whether it's possible to orgasm whilst kissing someone but I was close right then. In fact, I've just googled it and apparently it is possible to orgasm without touching anything... Try it ladies!

The kiss was so sensual, but not in a lustful rebound kind of way, more in an *oh my goodness I think I could spend my life with you,* kind of way.

He let my lips go and began walking away, but I stayed firmly where I was.

Uhhh. Decisions. Was it slutty to run after him and try to take him home with me and show him how I really felt? That stigma of being deemed a slut if you chase after a guy too quickly is something that I don't really agree with. If it's love, why should that be labelled as slutty? I know if gender roles were reversed, that whole stigma would be a lot different. Sorry - I seem to have gone off on a little societal rant here! Or was it just my horny hormones going crazy because he was this hot guy who cared about me and wiped my mascara stained face when I cried? As I looked up, he had stopped walking and was staring at me from a few yards away.

My heart leapt out of my chest and my breasts rose up and down beneath my silk blouse with eager anticipation as to what his next move would be.

He raised his left hand in front of him and moved his index finger forwards and backwards, beckoning me towards him. I started walking towards him slowly, trying to be all sultry and sexy and carefully watching for any loose bits of cobble that might kill me on my way over to his safe arms.

"WOAH!!!" He yelped.

"Shit, what is it!?" I answered, my heart racing.

"Just watch you don't fall over again. I'd like to take you home with me in one piece if that's okay."

"Oh, you absolute knob! I thought it was something urgent!" I squealed, suddenly erupting with laughter.

As I reached him he pulled my arm around his back and he placed his along the base of my spine again, rubbing those damn circles. Whatever this guy did he had me in pieces.

"Oh, but first, I'm taking you dancing." Freddie said, and pulled me towards a vibrant, bouncy club across the street.

As we walked into the club, there was some 90s

Vengaboys playing and Freddie smoothly got us in through security within a matter of seconds – the locals obviously knew him. He was gracious and thoughtful, and made sure to say hello and greet everyone.

As we reached the dancefloor, the DJ switched on a song that obviously suggested the universe was working in my favour. "Hot in Here" by Nelly blasted from the speakers, and all I could think was, yes, it is hot in here, please Fred, take off all your clothes...

Freddie knew how to move his hips and I was attempting to dance in some sort of rhythm, swaying my hair so that it caught in the neon light beams.

He kissed me again under the flashing colours and took my breath away.

Chapter 8

POSY

Love making, heart breaking, soul shaking...

After our sweaty bodies had danced until the early hours of the morning, we reached the hotel Freddie was staying in, and my stomach started doing somersaults – the good kind, not the pre-diarrhea food poisoning *oh my god I'm going to shit my pants,* kind. We hurried up to his apartment, taking the stairs because the elevator was like waiting for paint to dry. Though come to think of it, the wait for that elevator could have been worth it... He smoothly keyed his card which magically opened the door to his place and we clumsily fell over the threshold, the anticipation for what was to happen soon taking over our sensibility.

It was pitch black in the room and so Fred fumbled for the light switch, but after about five minutes he still couldn't find it and by that point the temptation was too much, and it overtook my entire body.

I threw my arms around his neck and he grabbed my bum pulling me up into what can only be described as some sort of spider monkey hold. My legs spread apart around him, my short skirt riding up, encasing his accommodating legs. He was just the perfect height for me and I for him.

A friend of mine, Scarlett, had once told me how awkward it was dating someone smaller than you because of the lack of positions in the bedroom thus available – and to be honest, Hamilton wasn't that much taller than me, so this whole being lifted up by a six-foot male was new, and very exciting.

Still holding me close, he pushed me up against the wall and started to move the passionate kisses from my lips, across to my earlobes and downwards to my neck. I urged him not to stop and he kept making satisfactory groans and it sure was doing the trick in turning me on even more than I thought was humanly possible. We still had our clothes on at this point and even while clothed we had this connection, this electricity holding us together.

He slowly let my legs drop down and I was stood up against the wall, his legs right up against mine, his breath on my ruffled pre-sex hair.

"Just know that I don't usually do this... and I know it's only the second date, but I have never looked at someone before and instantly felt something that I couldn't just walk away from. Is this okay, what I'm doing?" He asked in a gentlemanly manner.

"Is it okay? Honey it's *more* than okay."

He smiled cheekily and began unbuttoning my blouse, my red bra slowly coming into view. *Good choice* I noted, my little boobs looked fabulous if I did say so myself. He pushed my blouse downwards so that it clung onto my elbows and his kisses continued onto my breasts and lingered there for a few moments, his kisses switching from urgency back to soft and delicate motions. I began motioning my hand down towards his crotch, feeling him and slowly unzipping his superbly tight jeans, but he stopped me abruptly with his hand and said, "Ladies first."

Woah. Talk about a gentleman. Hamilton wouldn't even have sex unless it involved a starter of a hand job, and a dessert of a blow job. Here *I* was being treated. Seriously, I wondered, where had this guy been my whole life? And why the hell had I settled for a self-centered prick beforehand?

Fred guided me towards his bed, kissing me along the way.

He laid me down on the bed and slowly – standing

at the base of the bed - began unbuttoning his shirt. Undoing each button one by one, he revealed a chest crafted out of pure gold, but not a full on six pack, just a good manly bod – he had me in the palm of his hand. He kept his jeans on and climbed on top of me; Little Fred making an indent in the tightness of my stretched skirt.

Speaking of my skirt – that was the next item to be removed. Freddie gripped onto the elasticated waist and seductively and ever so carefully pulled it down past my thighs, my knees and over my toes, making sure to run his fingers along the important, sensitive parts.

My red laced knickers stuck out like a sore thumb amongst the grey, silk sheets and were yet to come off. It was a game of teasing one item at a time, almost like Strip Poker, but boy would I be playing it over and over again. Come to think of it, the only card game I can play is 'Snap' because '21' frankly requires too much mathematics to class it as a game, and not homework.

On top of me now, he stroked his fingers across my breasts and down the dip in the middle of my stomach, making his way down beneath the red lace. He kissed me hard just as I was about to sigh with pleasure and I could feel him enjoying it as much as I could.

Just as I was close, I pulled myself upright and gripped my hands hard around his neck, kissing him with sheer desperation and want for more. But it was his turn.

I pushed him towards where I had been lying, and climbed on top of him. Again, Hamilton wasn't the type of guy who enjoyed looking at the ceiling.

I straddled myself across him and craftily kissed him whilst undoing his jeans. Shuffling backwards I pulled his jeans down to reveal his black Calvin's that gave away his desire. Pealing them back, I nearly salivated.

Well let's just say that the masterpiece of the face was reciprocated in the pants department. He had an unopened condom box on his bedside table and he began opening one, rolling it out, but I stopped him. "It's ok, I'm on the pill." I said, when in actual fact I wasn't because I didn't need any type of contraceptive.

"Are you sure? I don't mind."

I kissed him, "Promise."

I'd had a rare form of leukemia as a child, and the chemo had resulted in my infertility. Hamilton hadn't minded as he didn't want kids anyway, but I had.

Hamilton was never open to adopting – he said that if he ever did have kids, he wanted them to have his good genes like the cock he is. I didn't want to stop the moment with Freddie with my sad childhood survival story, and so I skipped the truth.

I kissed Freddie gently and held him until he was nearly ready. He sat up and kissed me, scraping his hands through my hair. We sat kissing like that for a long time – me still in my netted lingerie, and he now fully naked beneath me.

I stood up at the end of his bed and bent forwards towards him, releasing my bra as I did. As they fell forward, he pulled me towards him, my nipples hardening against his touch. He gripped onto my knickers and pulled them down towards my ankles, but before he pulled them all the way he asked again if it was ok, and that we could stop there if it was too soon.

I giggled in a very giddy, teenager kind of way, and whispered, "Well we wouldn't want Little Fred to be disappointed for the *second* night running, now would we?" and stroking my fingers through his hair, he had my confirmation and his eyes spoke thousands of words.

He stood up and pushed up against me, holding me in his arms, our bodies naked but not yet at one.

I used my hands to guide him on top of me on the bed, and for a while he just kissed me whilst lying *just* above me, making sure I could feel how much he wanted to be with me. Pulling back from a lengthened kiss, he lingered close to my face and said, "You are so beautiful."

Again, he kissed me, and this time I parted my legs slightly, allowing him nearer to where I wanted him to be. But he took his time and complimented every part of me before he asked again if I was okay with it all happening so soon.

"God yes," I gasped, and pulled him so that he was touching me, ready for the big move. I was pulsing deep within and wanted him so badly.

"I get the feeling that even though this is our first time, it won't be our last," he hoarsely whispered, and then without hesitation he pushed himself softly inside me, and all at once I was moving back and forth with him, slowly and tenderly, our bodies groaning in pure ecstasy.

"Oh my god Fre-" I began and then screamed with pleasure as he moved his hips a little faster and moved me onto my side, continuing in his skillful ways. As he slowed I breathlessly asked, "Where have you been all my life Freddie?" and he replied "Ditto," with a hard yet fond kiss, pushing my arms above my head, kissing the sensitive areas that I wanted him too.

I lifted my neck up slightly to see and feel his beautiful buttocks on top of me, quickening again. I could feel his breath, warm and sharp against my chest and he pushed one last, beautiful, stretched stroke inside me and I tightened, becoming his.

He stayed inside me as I pulsed in satisfactory

intervals, as he stuck to his promise of "Ladies First" and let himself go after me. Moaning in satisfaction he pressed his mouth against me and then, after a few minutes of coming back down from the highest I'd ever been taken, he began making love to me again, and again, and again...

~

I woke up still lingering in my post coital satisfaction, and gleefully grinned to myself that I had found Freddie. He was fast asleep next to me, the cool sheets just covered his magical wand that had taken me for a ride to Hogwarts and back four times the night before. Oh my gosh, I've just laughed out loud writing that sentence. You know you're getting desperate with avoiding using the word penis when you start referring to it as the 'magical wand'.

Abrafuckingdabra.

I turned over to face him and cheekily ran my fingers beneath the covers, holding him and stroking him.

He opened one eye and gazed at me satisfactorily, "Are you ready for the next round already?" he said and pulled me out of bed, carrying me towards the shower.

Climbing in, we made love against the marbled cubicle, the water streaming and trickling down our shoulder blades, our kisses becoming more and more familiar with one another. Just a tip - shower sex is not as elegant as they make it out to be in the movies. You can just constantly hear your bum cheeks making farting noises against the window pane. We both had the giggles so much that we just stopped, him still inside me, our necks wrapped around one another, in complete hysterics. I'm not saying that it didn't end satisfactorily, despite the giggling interval...

~

After our shower, we sat on the balcony and had breakfast. Fred had made some blueberry pancakes (a guy that could cook, jeez, I was being given a Golden-Ticketed Wonka bar for sure) and even made my coffee just right, without me having to tell him how I took it.

We both began speaking at the same time, "Last night was-"

He interrupted so that he could say it first, "-like something I never knew even existed... I didn't want to stop.

I just utterly adore you. Every part of you Posy. And I know this sounds so strange because I've only known you for three days but honey, you've got me for life if you want me."

I blushed. I never blush. Like ever.

"I know!" I replied, "Before I met you, I was so lonely... I've never found someone like you before. Everything you do, you just know me somehow."

He kissed me softly in reply and I ran my fingers along the back of his neck – I pulled away gently and asked, "How about today, we get to know each other a little more? I want to know everything about you."

His face shifted slightly into nervousness and then back into *that* smile, "Okay you, but first how about I help you out of that little pair of shorts..."

~

I called in sick at work (not completely a lie, I was as lovesick as they come) and Fred luckily didn't have another concert until the end of the week. Plus, Andy the waiter knew the real reason for my absence and he encouraged it - he was the best boss ever.

I had Face Timed Jodie (who was on the toilet at the time, yet still answered) to explain all and she said she too had met someone unexpectedly, and would most probably be out all day too! Fancy that.

Barcelona was obviously Cupid in disguise for us both.

When Freddie and I managed to put some clothes on, we headed South towards the little old towns of Barcelona. Freddie drove as I took on the role of radio-channel controller.

Freddie was in amazement as to how many songs I knew, and laughed at my attempt to sing along with the power ballads, in particular "Nothing's Gonna Stop Us Now" by Starship. Then Freddie was in fits of laughter when Boys II Men's "I'll Make Love to You" came on and in the chorus, I kept rapping, well, attempting to rap!

I was in truth rather sore down there. But it was the sexiest type of sore. You girls know what I'm talking about.

We stopped for lunch at a little café, blessed with architecture worth stopping and taking a mental image of. It's funny how when you're young you don't appreciate the sincere beauty of a building, and then suddenly you just *see* what everyone else is stopping to look at – then again, I am an absolute geek, but not as full-on a geek as the human encyclopedia that I call my brother.

We didn't say a word as we orgasmed over the freshness of the salad leaves, and the garlicky-tomato pasta.

After we'd finished satisfying ourselves over our shared foodie characteristic, we made our way down to the water's edge, found a rock and perched down on it.

"So..." Fred said, "My life has been complicated

from the beginning – I'll try to make it as understandable as I can."

His eyes, glazed, looked straight ahead into the distance, as he recalled his childhood.

"My birth mom was a drug addict who cared for Heroin more than me. I never knew who my Dad was, and still don't to this day. My Mum took me to the sitter's one Sunday afternoon, and she never came back for me. I went straight into foster care."

Fred took a deep breath, and so did I. Behind everyone's exterior, there's always a profounder story than we anticipate.

"I was thirteen months old when I was adopted by Indra, the lady I adored and called Mum. My band is called *The Rainer's* because of her; in Hinduism her name means the warrior God of rain. Indra was a thirty-year-old something who'd waited around for ten years for The One to turn up... Indra, or Indi as many called her, having so much love in her heart, and running out of time with sheer impatience, adopted me. Funnily enough, a year later, my adoptive Mum, Indi, met the guy of her dreams.

A total hippie with hair down to his hips, and a year later I was officially adopted by him, and he's been like a Dad to me from the day he took my Mum under his wing."

I giggled, "Hehe, parents and their hippie stages eh!

My Mum is still stuck in that stage actually..."

He looked away from the ocean line and smiled at me, before continuing, "Childhood was lovely don't get me wrong, but my dyslexia held me back a lot. I got bullied, and I had no confidence at all – that's still a major problem for me even to this day. And it only got worse; Mum died when I was twelve. She went into hospital with a headache and came home with the news that she had a brain tumor, and had weeks, if that, to live. She died a week later. I loved my Mum so much. I looked up to her, she inspired me and motivated me, and told me I could when I thought I couldn't or wouldn't ever be able to do anything. She taught me how to face life with nothing but a smile. She was more my Mum than my birth Mum would ever be."

"Oh my gosh, I don't know what to say. Honey, I'm so sorry. I'm so, so sorry... Life's shit sometimes, isn't it?" I soothed, rubbing my thumb over his knuckles, seeing the passion in his eyes.

"Yes, life is shit, isn't it? And when it rains it pours, but you just have to keep going. Without my Dad, I really wouldn't have been where I am today. After

Mum died I went to a really dark place, and it took me a long while to find my way back up to the surface. Then, Posy, I met you and I found a little light in the tunnel."

I held him – I held him for so long because I just

didn't know what to say. There I was, brought up by two loving parents who, sure, had their ups and downs, but Fred – Fred had lived through abandonment, death and his own depression. God, I had a lot to be thankful for – in particular, the guy sat next to me on that rock. My rock.

I told him about my Mum and Dad and their near divorce, and he listened intently. I wasn't used to having someone's full attention, Hamilton would just nod and said, "Mm, yeah sounds great" to mostly anything I said.

But Fred, he was something else.

I explained more about Hamilton's dick move, and he sighed with disappointment at how appalling some people can be.

But he also said something rather spectacular; that he was glad that Hamilton had broken my heart. He told me that his Mum had always told him that sometimes you have to get your heart broken, so that someone else can come along and fix it.

He was my eternal fixer. My Bob the Builder.

I told him about the silliest of childhood memories, how I adored my geeky brother more than life itself, and how since I was a little girl I had wanted to be driven by Prince Charming, but not in a carriage, in a Corvette. That's what you get for having a Dad as a vintage car collector.

He smiled at me adoringly as memories dripped out of me, filling his cup of knowledge about the blonde before him, who was falling more and more in love with him and life itself.

I also told him the truth about the night before, and how my childhood cancer had resulted in me being sterile. I apologized for lying about being on the pill and explained how I hadn't wanted to have ruined the moment, because I really wanted to be with him. He held me in his arms, kissing the top of my head and replied, "That doesn't matter to me. You're here right now. That's *all* that matters. We can figure out the future later."

~

After our heart to heart and his gentle storytelling of his past, I fell even more in love with him.

This guy had a genuinely good heart, and eyes that spoke capacities; he had this warm intent inside his irises.

We made our way back to my apartment and clumsily both fell in through the door – Fred trying

to be a gentleman and allow me to go in first and me teasing him, hoping that Jodie wouldn't be home so that we could make good use of the furniture.

Erupting through the door we were greeted by a totally unexpected scene.

Jodie and Natalie were lying naked on the sofa.

I stood speechless, not really knowing how to handle the situation before me. I just wasn't expecting it. Jodie and Nat stared right back at me, sheer embarrassment on both of their faces. Fred quickly placed his hands over my eyes and shouted "Don't worry guys, we're leaving. Carry on where you left off."

Then I suddenly stopped in my tracks and I clicked why all those years ago Jodie had rejected my brother when I'd tried to set them up – she liked women! And why she never told me about her sex life. Ah, it all makes sense now. I took Fred's hands away from my eyes, and looked at Jodie and Nat who had now covered themselves with my huge crocheted throw.

Who doesn't want a lesbian best friend?

I mean, you don't need to worry about them ever running off with your boyfriend. I was still speechless and on the verge of bursting out into laughter at what Fred and I had walked in on.

"I'm so sorry to interrupt ladies." I said, an accepting smile travelling from my lips to Jodie's – our friendship was everlasting and it didn't change a thing. Fred's hand was resting on my bum, and he respectfully moved his hand up to the lower curve of my spine. I smiled shyly, and said to Jodie and Nat that we would leave them to it.

I pulled Fred's hand, guiding him towards the door and he shouted, "Nice to meet you Jodie."

As we shut the apartment door, Fred said "Did you not know?"

"No, I had no idea! We've been friends since childhood and I never even thought... Wait, you knew all this time?" I said as I turned to see a cheeky grin on his face.

"Oh god yes, Nat has been talking non-stop about Jodie since Day 1. You can tell by the way they look at each other. It's the same as the way I look at you when you're not looking."

"Oh, I could kiss you all day... Why are you so sweet?"

"Well, because I'm made of honey." He said, laughing at his own clever and bloody cheesy reply. The type of corny humour that was the good kind.

"You utter weirdo," I said laughing, "Mm I could just eat some honey drizzled on top of something."

"Well, I can arrange that for sure," He replied cheekily, turning my words into the most congenial euphemisms.

He pressed me up against the wall kissing me slowly and hard, teasing me with his tongue because he knew it made me tick.

"I'm sooooo hungry," I said, teasing him more.

"Oh yeah, what do you fancy baby?" He said, running his hand down the back of my neck.

"Erm... a panini?" I whispered, interrupting our little verbal sexting session.

"Sorry little Freddie, but Posy's hungry." I said, chuckling as he winked at me.

"She might be hungry later." Freddie said, looking down and talking to his pants. He's so funny and strange. I loved him.

Chapter 9

POSY

My hair fell out

I remember the moment my hair started to fall out quite vividly.

When I was about thirteen I had started with banging headaches, and after visiting the doctor's numerous times, and them telling me it was just a hormonally induced migraine, I decided to get a second opinion.

That second opinion told me it wasn't migraines at all, after a brain scan they found that I had a rare form of lymphoma in my pituitary gland. Suddenly I was this girl not only with new pointy things growing out of her chest, but also one with cancer.

I remember Noah's face when the doctor had broken the news to us, he'd been unreactive. Mum and Dad had howled, crying their souls out as they feared my diagnosis, but Noah was different. Noah made me immediately feel as if it wasn't as big a deal as everyone was making it out to be. He told me he would do everything he could to fix me.

And I'm so glad he did, because I'm pretty sure I wouldn't have made it through all of the treatment without his constant positivity. That's one of the many reasons that I adore him.

A week after my diagnosis which was classed as being stage 3 (AKA the stage before they define you as being terminal), I started a new form of chemo that only three people had tried beforehand. The results of the chemo drug trials hadn't been entirely positive, I was told, but it was my only hope.

I was told the side effects were really quite cruel, and that long term they would ruin all of my chances of ever having a baby. But I had ignored every negative and tried to focus on the positive – which was living.

My chemo was pretty easy at first. I just got the occasional bout of sickness or the odd rash on my inner elbow. Noah would sit with me whilst the doctors injected me hourly, with a daily dose of a whole mashup of ingredients that would make me better.

He was, and still is my rock. He usually insisted on reading his Dr Who magazines to me. to which I gave him the finger. He was a typical annoying brother, caring and irritating as hell. Love him.

But then, a month after my first 28-day course of treatment, I woke up with a huge fur ball of hair on my pillow.

My Mum and Dad had informed the school about my diagnosis, but I had decided that I'd rather the whole school not know and so just the important teachers were told. But when I lost my hair, I was called names by so many mean people, taunting that I looked like a boy...

Noah didn't like seeing me emotionally in pain as well as physically. And besides, the doctors had told me that school may well and truly go out of the window because health came first – but as you know me pretty well by now, if I want something I'll do it. So, I continued with school from home and each teacher Skyped me with all the work I needed to catch up on.

My whole body started reacting to the drugs after the first month and I had to be drip fed for weeks on end, because my stomach couldn't support anything I consumed.

My Mum could not cope with any of it – seeing her little girl cooped up in a hospital bed whilst all of the other kids my age were out partying, or chasing after their first crushes. I can't even imagine what it must feel like.

Whilst I was in hospital, I befriended a fairly oldish man called Nicholas, who was in having treatment for prostate cancer. He and I spoke regularly whilst we were being pumped with various drugs, and almost looked forward to our treatment, in gratitude for the company of someone who really knew how you were feeling.

And you'll never guess who just so happened to be Nicholas's young daughter... that's right – Jodie.

Jodie and I were brought together because of cancer, and I think the strong force of it made our own friendship that little bit tougher.

After a while, Jodie would come to the hospital not only to visit her Dad, but also to visit me and it blossomed from there.

She was in the year above, and as you'll all know if you've been to an all-girls high school; being friends with someone in the year above is frankly unheard of. It's like a crime against the school code.

But Jodie and I were rebellious in that way, and somewhat outcasts... we clicked and that was that. She was there for me when I needed a friend. A *real* friend.

After a few months of friendship, the worst and the inevitable happened.

Nicholas didn't show up for treatment one day. He'd fallen asleep the night before and not woken up the next morning.

I remember my whole life flashing before my eyes as I sobbed over losing someone who understood what was going on inside my body, and I was so scared about the possibility that it could have potentially been me.

I hurt deeply for Jodie who had lost her Dad. You can't ever prepare for that.

Though Mum and Dad insisted that I didn't, I managed to persuade Noah to take me to Nicholas's funeral.

I felt it was my duty to both him and Jodie who had been my absolute rocks when I felt as if I was about to drown in the cancerous ocean.

I recall being wheeled into the church, a sea of faces and black clothes pitying me and my bald, slightly fluffy head.
Noah stood beside me, his hand resting on my frail and fragile shoulder – I had expected myself to be an absolute mess, but I wasn't.

I shed some tears, but I also tried to concentrate on the positives... on the fact that I had been blessed with a friendship with him, and because of him. Nicholas had told me that he knew in his heart that I could fight anything in the world, and that had been a phrase that I would concentrate on when the needle hurt too much, or when the sickness was too much to handle.

My concentration turned to Jodie who was an absolute wreck during the service. I hugged her for what felt like a thousand years until she stopped crying, and began finding reasons to laugh. It took a long while, but like she had gotten me through my worst moments, I somehow managed to help her, just a fraction, with her own battles.

After an entire year of battling a disease that had very nearly removed the life from my bones, I was classed as being in remission; and six months later I was free from any cancerous cell. It was a miracle. The only side effect I had walked away with was a new shorter hairstyle, and an inability to have any babies in the future.

I counted myself lucky for still walking away with breath in my lungs and a beat in my heart, but a selfish part of me had always longed for having my own family.

But as Jodie has always said, "Sometimes shit happens for reasons unexplained. And sometimes those reasons manage to sort themselves the fuck out."

Any type of advice given by Jodie usually has a fuck thrown in there. Because, why the fuck not?

Chapter 10

JODIE

The L Word

I'd known for years that it wasn't men that did it for me. In fact, I think the first time I knew was when I watched a chick flick at the movies when I was about thirteen and felt more for the female lead, than the male that Posy had been obsessing over at the time.

I guess in a way that's why I had my slutty years in high school – because I feared people knowing the real me. Instead I invented this other persona and I fooled around with every living male that entered my life, to try and hide how I was really feeling.

My Mum and Dad had not always been positive with their views towards homosexuals... they seemed to be stuck in this era of lesbians being a word you whispered, instead of shouted out loud proudly from the hilltops.

I had always wanted to tell Posy, I really had, but there had always been this worry inside me that if I told her she'd freak and think I was into her. Don't get me wrong, she's so very pretty, but just because she's a female doesn't mean I'm going to go and jump on top of her. There was just this insecure feeling inside of me that didn't want to ruin a masterpiece of a friendship. And so, in a way, I was pretty relieved that Posy had found out the way she did... because she had no other choice but to believe it. Her accepting smile had said a lot, and I immediately felt this sense of relief and thankfulness that I had a friend like her. Without her, life wouldn't be quite worth living.

Her new fella had reacted pretty well too and I had liked him immediately. He looked after Posy like a guy should, he always had his hand hovering at the base of her back in a really sweet, healthily protective way. And trust me, I'm no romantic but those two had something rather special. I'd known that since the first night I'd opened my big mouth and shouted out his name... *totally* not on purpose, may I add...

Truth be told, I'd been scheming with Natalie in setting up Fred and Posy for a good few months beforehand, and ironically during the process I fell head over heels for Nat.

She'd been just what I was looking for, and everything I knew I would ever need. And she was the first person that made me feel normal for feeling the way I do. I was just waiting for the right time to tell Posy, but then the surprise meeting occurred and I'm pretty glad it did. Life can get tiring when you keep hiding from reality.

Posy had kindly said that Natalie and I were welcome to stay at her apartment seeing as she and Freddie didn't mind sharing the same bed. Goarrrrnnnn Posy!!

I still couldn't believe that Posy had walked on us in the act... literally, what a way to find out! Fred's reaction had said it all – he'd known all along; Posy however was a little more surprised at the revelation. But her friendly smile had made me feel silly for not telling her sooner.

I guess I'd just been afraid that she would no longer want to be friends with me. Silly I know, but I was brought up in a way that made me feel as if it wasn't the right way to feel.

Posy and Freddie started double dating with Nat and I, and it was as if everything had fallen into place for all of us, finally.

Freddie invited us all over to his one night, and he managed to wrap me right around his little finger.

He'd prepared a fully vegan meal as Posy had mentioned that I was one, and had taken the time to research every single ingredient to make sure that I could eat it. There's something about a guy that actually listens, it makes you like them that little bit more.

The second double date had, however, proved disastrous, darling. I'd invited Natalie, Posy and Freddie to a PRIDE march in the center of Barcelona. I had left them all coffeeing in a coffee shop, as I had wanted to go and get involved in the center of the action. Posy had warned me to behave as I'd had three beers and she knew what a nuisance I was if I drank a bit too much – recall the gay paramedic story? Hashtag wonky nose over here.

I headed over to grab a protest sign, and suddenly felt a rough hand grip my shoulder.

"Excuse me, are you gay?" the plump policeman asked me.

"Yes, I am. Why – you got a problem with that?"

"No Miss, but I was just saying to my friend here that you won't suck his dick because you're gay."

It really riled me up and so I replied with, "I wouldn't suck your dick if you were the last person on earth."

"Well how about if I take you down to the station, would you really not suck his dick in return for me not arresting you?"

"No, I fucking wouldn't because I don't like dickheads like you."

And just before I did what I was about to do, I imagined "I Fought the Law" by The Clash being played in the background. I couldn't help but swing my arm up and hit him hard on the nose, leaving him with blood oozing out of his nostrils. He had hurt me with his words.

And then all at once he was hitting me back and pushing his knee into the base of my back, grinding my face into the hard concrete. Thumping and thumping, kicking and attacking me.

Suddenly a blur of men dressed in shades of blue came over to me, grabbing hold of my arms and pinning me down, "Madam, you've just assaulted a police officer. You are under arrest."

Hearing the screeching of sirens, Posy, Freddie and Natalie came running out onto the street, seeing me bloody, battered and bruised, being dragged away towards a police car.

~

An hour later, I managed to get myself my right of a

phone call.

I rang Posy.

"Oh, my goodness, Jodie, is that you? Are you ok? What happened? Oh my god we have all been so worried about you – but they wouldn't tell us anything."

"Well that's because those fuckers made fun of me for being gay and then made me angry so I hit them, but then they kept on hitting me and hitting me."

"Oh Jodie, honey. That's totally out of order. We'll sort this, promise… oh Natalie wants to speak to you Jodie, just hold on a moment…"

And then a very upset sounding Natalie answered the phone, "Oh Jodie, I've been so worried about you. What they did to you isn't right at all baby. We'll get through this together, and Jodie… I love-…" she said.

And then the phone line went dead as a dodo and I was left all alone, sat in a hot, sweaty cell with 50 other women. That usually would have been quite the fantasy for me, but well – the circumstances were a tad bit different, seeing as two of my ribs had been broken. And I couldn't even see out of one of my eyes.

At midnight, a police officer came in and said that I was free to go.

To be honest I was in pure shock. Whatever Posy had managed to do was pure magic – I knew from my law school days that assaulting a police officer in Spain could mean up to six months behind bars.

Carefully standing up, the pain unbearable in my stomach from all the kicks and punches, I made my way out of the cell and into the open air.

Posy, Natalie and Freddie were all stood outside, anticipating my discharge.

They all came over and hugged me one by one, Natalie gently pecking my blacked cheek with a kiss.

"Thank you, thank you, thank you guys so much. How did you manage to get me out?"

Posy and Natalie smiled and turned to Fred who was stood very shyly with his head down, not wanting to take credit for whatever he'd done.

"Tell her what you did Freddie." Posy said, prompting him to tell me how he'd managed to heroically save me.

"It was nothing really. I just tweeted about how angry I was and got loads of people to sign a petition…"

"…I found a guy who'd been videoing the march on his phone, and had caught you being assaulted by the police in the background. I shared it on all of my websites and word got around I suppose. Honestly, it's nothing..." He said, waving his hand in the air as if to dismiss his contribution.

I ran and leaped into Freddie's arms before saying, "Look mate, your *nothing* obviously has a different definition to what I'd constitute as nothing. Thank you, thank you, thank you."

And then I gave him a great, big, giant kiss on the lips. I think his eyes nearly burst out of his skull.

"Ah I'm a lesbian Freddie, treat it as a compliment."

Freddie's eyes were still wide with astonishment, and then we all burst out laughing, well that was until I realized how painful it was to laugh with two broken ribs. And so off to the hospital we went!

Chapter 11

POSY

Ireland is Gas!

When booking my flight from France to Gatwick after my tragic experience with Theo and Café Formidable Guy, it was cheaper to get the ferry from Calais direct to Dublin for the night, and then fly to Gatwick from Dublin airport. And, being me, the cheapskate that I am, I went for the stop-over option!

Besides, I could tick it off my bucket list – and maybe even have my first taste of Guinness whilst I was at it. But the only problem was that I was both boat sick and afraid of anything that floats on water ever since I saw Titanic as a kid. I won't even go on a pedalo... On a canal... In England. I mean, what about sharks; have you *seen* Jaws?

The ferry across the water was an absolute nightmare. The waves seemed to be arguing with one another, pushing our boat like an opinion back and forth and to and fro. After very nearly throwing up my breakfast bar, I headed indoors to try and find a stable point that didn't make me feel as if I was well and truly pissed two times over.

I made my way into the little television room and fumbled to find the remote, switching on the power button. *Titanic* was the only film available on the satellite television. I am not even kidding you; it was the part where they hit the iceberg and then the boat starts filling up with water. I couldn't even distract myself with the beauty of Jack Dawson. That shit should be banned on any kind of boat. Good god. It was a long journey, but I made it out alive and the ship didn't sink. Positive, right?

My ferry from France to Dublin arrived at 9am, and my flight back from Dublin to Gatwick wasn't until 6pm that evening. So, I had an entire day to explore everything I possibly could in the beauty that was Ireland.

Everybody spoke so fast in Ireland, I mean, when I'm nervous I talk really fast and often get told to shut up, but this was another level of speed.

However, you've got to love an Irish accent even if you don't have a clue what they're saying half the time – total turn on in my eyes.

I walked out of the port, after leaving my baggage safely in a lockup and made my way to Dublin city center via the shuttle.

I grabbed a coffee and a croissant to go, took a tourist map and decided that I wanted to first go and visit the Dublin Writer's Museum. I was a typical lit geek since I had a sexy high school teacher who'd helped me to understand the real meaning of literature - plus he had my constant attention as he had the nicest arse you have ever seen...

The museum was magical; it was just so big. There were rows and rows of books, all neatly placed on antique, renaissance-inspired bookshelves. First editions of Hardy, Austen, Bronte and my all-time favourite Aphra Behn were displayed, and I was in total awe.

My brother's addiction was dinosaurs, and mine was purely literature – that place was my haven. I stayed there for hours, just taking in the mesmerizing space around me, until my transfixion was interrupted by a tap on my shoulder.

"Remember me?" the friendly voice behind me said, and as soon as I heard the Waterford twang I knew in an instant who it was.

"Dymphna! Oh, my goodness, it's been so long! How are you?" I exclaimed, violently hugging my old University friend.

Dymphna had been on my English Language and Literature course at Surrey Uni, and we'd been pals since I was eighteen – but then she'd gotten a job opportunity over the water, back in her hometown, and taken it.

"Oh Posy, I'm doing great thanks, it's so great to see you. How long are you here for lovely? Are you married? Have you got kiddies?" She questioned, enthusiastically.

My smile faded into a straighter line as I replied, "Just for the day... before my flight back home tonight, and nope, newly divorced and nil on the child tally."

"Oh honey, it's obviously his loss. I mean, you're so gas and beautiful!!"

I chuckled, "Gas? What does that mean?"

Dymphna was always teaching me her dialect ever since Uni, but 'gas' was a new one to add to my collection.

"Gas means... funny and quirky!" Dymphna excitedly explained, "Oh Posy, please tell me you'll spend the day with me? I'm off work this afternoon, and my little girl is at preschool until 4:30." She said, pulling my arm urging me to accept.

"Oh well, if you insist Dymphs, I'm in!"

~

We had lunch at a small café and chatted about old times, and recent events.

Dymphna was happily married to her lovely childhood sweetheart and had a gorgeous daughter. I felt my heart sink when I saw how happy she was, she had the life that I had planned for Hamilton and I, but my fairytale had frankly gone tits up.

I explained all about Hamilton's adventurous dick, and about the revelation where I had been confronted with the reality of the situation.

Just as we had finished lunch, the sun started to peek out through the clouds and so Dymphna and I jumped on the train, and made our way down to what was known locally as the Velvet Strand.

We both threw our shoes onto the sand, hitched our dresses up and ran like children (and Phoebe from *FRIENDS*) across the sand to the water. The sea was blue as blue, but the beach was empty; we had the place to ourselves.

Dymphs and I ran into the sea and spun around, our arms in the air, our heads staring up at the clouds. How magical a worry-free life can be when it's spent with friends who are just as crazy as you are.

We splashed about in the water and laughed until we cried.

"You know what, I don't want to see Ireland. I could

stay right here and be happy forever." I told
Dymphna.

After a while, we strolled along the beachfront, our
arms linked, speaking non-stop like old friends do,
and came across a very Irish looking bar to waste a
few hours in. I had my first pint of Guinness which
was utterly disgusting. It was like drinking thick
gravy granules mixed with a bit of moldy banana.
Not a fan, but hey, can't knock it until you've tried
it, right? I remember Hamilton saying the exact
same thing when trying to convince me into having
sex with him in the 'other hole'; "Can't knock it till
you've tried it Posy," he'd told me. And that's when I
had said, "Well I'll put an aubergine up your arse
and you can tell me how it feels." He never bought
any type of phallic vegetable following that
conversation.

At the pub, there was a local band singing "Love
You Till The End" and it made the hairs on the back
of my neck stand up. You can't beat the magical
vibes of Irish pub music – in fact, ever since I had
seen *P.S. I Love You*, I'd always hoped a guy would
come across the room and surprise me at the bar,
but it seemed Gerard Butler has got lost on his way
to find me.

Plus, all of the men in the bar we were in were
about sixty, pissed on Guinness, who could pass for
being nine months pregnant. But hey, you can't
meet a sexy guy in *every* bar, right?

With the band on their break, Dymphna and I made our way back down to the beachfront and with Dymphna being a local she was able to borrow a 90s boom box from the owner of the glorious pub, to take down with us.

After explaining the entire Hamilton drama, she had noted how I needed to dance it out of my system – shake out the heartbreak and renew my skin for a new love. It was her Irish tradition with every friend who had ever been heartbroken.

So, we jumped around in the sand to Kylie, Scouting for Girls and good ol' Lionel Richie. We looked like absolute nutcases but it was the first time I'd really felt happy since Hamilton. I was fed up of heartbreak and music has a way of curing the soul.

After walking with Dymphna to pick up her little girl from pre-school, we said our goodbyes and vowed we would do it again soon. After a teary cuddle, I headed back towards the port to collect my bags and then walked over to the airport.

The flight was on time which was utterly miraculous considering the state of my luck. That was until we got on the plane and a man remarked that one of the wings looked a little wonky. Talk about a woman already traumatized by her first ferry experience; this was just the icing on the cake.

After a long-awaited plane switch to an even shittier

propeller plane - which looked as if it was in fact a death machine - I landed home. I survived. I made it out alive. I'm practically Bear Grylls trained after that experience.

Chapter 12

FREDDIE

Touring

My band and I had started touring in 2015 and were due to finish our tour in Barcelona, where our main fan base was.

There was something quite breathtaking about an entire room of people screaming out the lyrics that you had once sat down to write. And it made all of the sleepless nights, the jetlag and the homesickness, worthwhile.

I wasn't interested in dating any of my fans because I wasn't the type of guy to sleep with someone and leave on a plane the next day. It just wasn't in my nature. Never has been.

I'd seen the true extent of why one-night stands were just not for me. I wasn't the type of guy who could just fuck and forget. And besides, the type of girls who just wanted to fuck me and not love me, weren't the type of girl I was truly looking for.

I was the quiet one in the band who would always leave the club early to go home and binge watch some Netflix extravaganza, trying to find inspiration from the characters. I always found that songwriting came to me in those moments when I felt alone, because it was when the emotions inside of me were raw, and real. I did Netflix and Chill, just by myself.

We'd been all over Europe gigging to crowds of screaming girls, and we were due to go to Ireland until Josh broke his arm falling off the stage. And a broken arm means a drummer is out of action. We'd been booked to play at this little Irish pub in the center of Dublin which was a place I had always wanted to go to.

I was a hopeless romantic, thinking I'd find my Rose like Jack did (though hopefully not die from frostbite in the process) or find my Holly like Gerry had.

I always got made fun of for going all *P.S. I Love You* when one of my bandmates tried to set me up with a girl for the night.

It just wasn't me. I wanted a Holly. A girl that wouldn't leave me in the morning; a girl who'd stick around for longer than the night.

Who knows. Maybe I would have met my Holly in Dublin if it hadn't had been for Josh breaking his arm. But hey, I thought, maybe Barcelona would be the place for me, and it was.

I tried to go back to Arizona whenever I could to visit my Dad – he'd been struggling with his health for a while and I felt bad that I couldn't be there to look after him as much as I wanted to.

I know Mum had told him that he should try and find someone after she'd died, but he said he'd been looking but couldn't find his Holly either. The truth is, Holly's are rare – if you manage to find one, don't let her go.

Another thing I struggled with was my confidence. I wasn't the best looking of guys in my eyes, even though my fans screaming out sexual references indicated differently.

I was just a regular guy with kind of shaggy hair and green eyes. I suffered with depression in my teenage years after being knocked down by too many people to count, which is probably why I have never really had a lot of self-esteem. Again, songwriting was my escape for that.

Chapter 13

POSY

Homeland

After the disastrous experience of being chased by pigs in France, and a quick stop off in Dublin, I returned to Kent for a few weeks to prepare myself for my next venture. After a long delayed, tiresome flight seated like a piggy in the middle between a Labour supporter and a Conservative enthusiast, I was pretty pleased to set my feet back down on my familiar homeland. It was a great start when my luggage was the only suitcase not going around on the circle, flat escalator – I don't have a clue what they're really called...

After a one-sided argument with one of the miserable passport security officers, they concluded that my luggage was still on the plane which was due to fly to South Africa at any minute. So, after a hectic dash across the airport to stop the plane from flying off with my essentials (which included my extra-large period knickers), I eventually made it out and into the Arrivals lounge.

I was greeted by Noah and his little rascals, who ran up to me and hung to my body like spider monkeys. Noah greeted me with the usual - a sloppy kiss on the forehead and said, "Nice to see you back home crazy old lady."

I laughed and said, "If it wasn't for my beautiful nephew and niece being in earshot right now, I would personally tell you to P-I-S-S off"
We both burst out laughing as Jessie said, "What does piss mean Aunty P?"
Just FYI, kids can spell swear words quicker than you think. We always did that, me and Noah, made each other laugh over the simplest of things. It was surreal returning back to a familiarity I had once took for granted.

Whilst walking towards the car park, the kids were babbling on to one another. I wondered why Iz wasn't there. I didn't want to assume but I got the feeling that Iz was one of *those* mums.

But Noah seemed pretty happy most of the time, though I did notice he wasn't as upbeat with the kids as he usually was.

He was typically one of those Dads that was constantly doing silly impressions of their favourite book characters, or lifting them high in the sky, and spinning them around like human helicopters.

"Where's Iz, is she waiting in the car?" I asked. Noah told me she was working overtime at the hospital again to help pay for the kids' school fees. I didn't really comprehend it. If it was over me being able to spend more time with my kids and send them to a free school I think I would. I wouldn't want to miss out on precious moments. I went to a crappy high school and didn't turn out too bad, right?

As it was the school holidays when I returned home, Noah had planned that we drove straight from the airport down to see Mum and Dad – maybe spend a few nights down at the B&B. With the kiddos, but minus Izzy.

I hadn't seen Mum and Dad since the divorce as I had literally booked my ticket to France a few weeks after it had been finalised.

Mum was rather quirky like me, the type who dressed in flowy skirts and bohemian blouses, with those trainers that have a huge, bouncy sole. She was an absolute health freak and was regularly emailing me with vouchers for Holland and Barrett. She even sent me cruelty free vaginal lubricant made of nettle and kale in the post once. Who in their right mind puts a nettle anywhere near their vajayjay?

I love my Mum in every possible way – she's an absolute nutcase, don't get me wrong, her only flaw is always seeing the best in everyone (and being best pals with Hamilton's bitch of a mother). For example, when Hamilton cheated on me and I rang them up to inform them about what had happened, Mum had said, "Look, sweetie, lots of men do this, and sometimes they're just a bit lost you know?"

I remember laughing out loud and replying, "Lost Mum? *Fucking* lost? Well, he certainly knew how to find his penis and stick it in her-" but I was cut off by Noah removing the phone from my grasp. I was angry and hungry at the time – not a good mix for any woman - and had a bit of an outburst. I had just blown my fuse, which doesn't happen often. Promise.

Dad on the other hand was the opposite of Mum – he was the type of man who practically wore the same outfit every day, bar a change of different coloured socks. His dress sense was pretty bland compared to Mum's, but his personality and cooking certainly were not.

Dad was the type of guy who knew me inside and out, and was the one who stayed at home when we were younger whilst Mum worked over time despite being financially stable without it; hence why I have this Room 101 issue with Mums who choose to work overtime when they don't really need to.

As we were walking over to the car, Jessie and Niall suddenly showed signs of excitement, and Noah had a hint of a smile creeping through his friendly lips.

"Sooooo... there's a new member in the family Posy." Noah said, one hand on each of the kiddie's shoulders.

Noah opened the boot and out popped a beautiful little black puppy dog, with the biggest brown eyes you've ever seen.

"Oh, my goodness he's beautiful!" I cooed, running over to snuggle the bouncy bundle, "But how are you going to have time for a puppy you guys?"

"Well," Noah said, "that's another thing that's kind of a surprise; I've decided to become a stay at home Dad and work part time from home, my business is going really well and I don't want to be working full time when I don't need to... Life goes by too quickly."

I smiled. My comments about Izzy had obviously hit home and he'd made his move.

"And what is this little fella called?" I asked my

gorgeous niece and nephew intriguingly, swiftly changing the subject.

"Well, Jessie wanted to call him Bum Bum but I said no Jessie that's a very silly name and we are growed up now, so we decided to name him Bob – because that's a growed up name isn't it Aunty Posy."

I laughed out loud thinking only my nephew and niece would come up with that.

"You guys called him Bob? Well what a handsome Bob he is!"

Every couple of hours driving along the motorway we pulled into services to a) let Bob wee, b) let the kids wee and c) get FOOD and COFFEE for the adults.

The drive down was glorious and reminded me of the trips we used to take with Dad, when Mum was away working.

We would spontaneously decide to drive and see where the road took us on Friday nights, armed with a tent and a pop-up barbecue.

We enjoyed the simplicities of life. When we were younger we would play badminton, using the tent as our net – that was until we hit a shuttlecock too hard and it landed in someone's cup of tea. Good shot, though right?

And when we were older we would camp out beneath the stars, with Noah rambling on and trying desperately hard to interest me in his constellational knowledge. Sometimes we'd play cards, but as I've told you before, my card playing experience begins and finishes with Snap. We just enjoyed every minute of it, and I wouldn't have changed it for the world.

~

We arrived at Mum and Dad's B&B at around 6pm, and the winter sun was just setting beneath the midst of the foggy backdrop. Mum had said that another surprise person had booked in to stay at the B&B last minute, and we would all be having dinner with them later on.

Oh gawd, the last time Mum had given me a surprise was when she tried to set me up with a far from straight gardener who frankly spoke higher than a boy pre-puberty. Which is high let me tell you. Helium high.

Noah asked Mum and Dad to babysit the kids and we took a walk with Bob up to a little castle, about a half mile along a country road. We perched on the edge of a fractured rock and Bob lay down beside us, teething on his lead.

Noah popped his arm around my neck and pulled me into a brotherly hug, and kissed the side of my forehead lovingly. As we had been walking up to the castle, Noah had been trying to tell me all about the cliff face and its exfoliation and quantification and blah blah blah blah blah. He always tells me off for having selective hearing when he goes off on a geographical tangent – but I love him even more for his geekiness, I just don't need to learn the meaning of the word quantification before I die...

"I've missed you sis. How's it hanging Mrs?" Noah asked me, his sandy hair blowing gently in the southern wind. The sun was hiding behind the clouds, momentarily providing a little warmth to my bare skin.

"I'm okay. I'm alright," I said shrugging my shoulders with average approval about my own personal happiness, and added, "It's not easy being single *and* divorced at twenty-six, but you know. I've got an alright brother - I *suppose* that's something to smile about." I laughed, nudging him.

He gazed at me admirably, he was always telling me how proud he was to be my brother because it meant that unlike friends, we shared a part of each other. He slowly nodded in reply to my words and hugged me again.
"It'll all work out. Just don't date anyone remotely associated with professionally being a Twat, alright?" he said, and we both burst out laughing.

"Uh god I know. I made that mistake in France," I told him. "Slept with a guy who I thought was single, who then came in to the café where I was working the next day to be seated with his wife and two children. I felt awful, but I got my revenge..."

"Oh, what is it with guys hurting my little sister... And, oh god Posy, what did you do?" Noah asked, slightly concerned at my mischievous, psycho smile.

"Well, I gave him some sleeping pills and then I grabbed a knife and I plunged it right into his balls, puncturing each one with hard blows."

"What the hell." Noah said holding painfully onto his trouser area, believing every word his silly sister said.

I left it a few moments before revealing my little, teeny weenie exaggerative lie.

"Did you actually believe me?!" I exclaimed, chuckling, "I promise you I didn't go all *Fatal Attraction* on him. I simply proved to him that he wasn't the best I'd ever had, by pretending to have sex by myself." Noah bent over laughing at my story, and it seemed as if it had been a long time since he'd *really* laughed.

We spent moments just staring out at the ocean

and at the views that we all forget are there for us to go and seek.

"Look Noah, I don't mean to be blunt, but where's Iz?"

He gulped, with a lump in his throat, and said, "Things aren't the best between us at the moment. I've tried to tell her that she's working too hard but she's said that that's her passion, and that I shouldn't be telling her what to do. That's why I brought the kids up to see Mum and Dad, and you, because their Mum isn't capable of doing her job right now."

I nodded slowly, taking in his words and thinking rationally about how to reply without being bias towards my brother's emotions.

"Just be patient Noah, she might just need some time to figure herself out. Just keep waiting. If you really love her, just believe in her decision okay?"

I gave him a big cuddle and reminding us it was time to go home, the heavens opened and poured down onto us. Poor little Bob was shivering uncontrollably, his ears sopping with raindrops as he experienced the lovely climate Britain had to offer.

We ran as fast as we could along the windy lane laughing at how each other's hair looked super sexy and wet, enjoying the cool droplets dripping onto us, reminding us of our youthful aliveness.

~

FYI Mum's 'surprise' she had organized was utter shit. The surprise guest was in fact Hamilton and his delightful bitch of a Mother, Judith. I pulled my Mum aside and asked what the hell was wrong with her brain, and why the hell she'd think Hamilton being there was a surprise, and not an absolute fucking nightmare.

She'd droned on about how second chances can never go amiss, and how it would be nice for him to see his niece and nephews.

Yeah right – the kids knew him off by heart as Uncle Knobhead.

My brother was fuming also, but I reminded him that we had to stay for the evening and making the situation even worse wasn't going to help anybody.

I avoided talking to Hamilton all evening, who was wearing ripped jeans that looked as if they belonged in the teenage girl's section at New Look. Talk about a midlife crisis in the making.

The kids were upstairs with Bobby the puppy and so I popped up to see them, laughing to myself as I went up each step at the sheer unbelievable situation that the apparent surprise had turned into.

As I walked into the spare room where Niall and Jessie were sat, I nearly went flying on an empty packet of Haribo.

"Oh God, what did you two do?" I asked as I walked into see a very hyper Bob doing laps around the room.

"Well, Daddy said to give him treats if he did any wee wees on that mat. So, we gave him Haribo each time he did it."

"Oh no," I said, kneeling next to them, "Sweeties aren't for doggies you guys, they have special treats – you see the ones up there in that jar?" I said, and pointed to the top of the bedside cabinet.

I rang Jodie up because she did a course once in animal care and something or other, and I figured she was much more trustworthy than asking Google.

Jodie said that he'd be fine, perhaps a little hyper, but it would all come out the other end. And it did. Explosively. Everywhere.

And so, me, Niall and Jessie sat on the floor keeping a beady eye on the crazy lunatic of a puppy legging it in circles around us.

I'd sat explaining to Jodie over the phone what my

Mother had organized, and her answer was indeed an expletive.

And then suddenly, I had an idea.

"You know, Hamilton always loved Haribo..." I said, and my little niece and nephew's ears pricked up as they suddenly realized what I was suggesting.

"I mean, I'm just saying – wouldn't it be a waste to leave all this Haribo lying around?" I said, pointing to a recent pile of poop with a Haribo love heart sticking out of it.

And so, being the sick and twisted ex-wife I am, I grabbed some disposable gloves and put a load of poopy Haribo into a bag. Then the kids went and delivered it to Hamilton like the sweet and innocent children I've brought them up to be. Never have I been so glad for a dog to have explosive diarrhea.

When I snuck into Noah's room to tell him, he did tell me off for getting the kids involved, but then congratulated me on my magnificent revenge on my dick of an ex-husband.

"You're such a bad influence on my children you know Posy – but they love you, and so do I, and I'm so glad you're training them to be just like you. Totally loveable and totally psychotic. The perfect combination."

Then, after an exhausting few hours of rooting through dog poop, Bob fell asleep on my belly, I fell asleep on Noah, Noah fell asleep with Jessie under his arm and Jessie fell asleep with Niall cuddling her. All I needed was right there on that bed and I was blissfully happy.

Chapter 14

POSY

A LOT Can Change

Fred and I spent the next few weeks together, falling more and more in love with one another – spending most nights dancing close to naked around the kitchen, to the likes of Barry Manilow and Bob Seger.

Fred practically moved into my apartment, and the surprising thing was, it felt so natural. There we were, two people who had met one night, slept together the next, and many, many more times the next day and the next... And somehow, it worked.

We hadn't argued or even bickered over one of us being a little bit late, or not keeping the apartment clean enough.

It seemed too good to be true, but it *was* true. I had landed flat on my feet, and I was determined for it to remain that way for the rest of my life.

Our lives just fitted together like fate had crafted them to; I worked late shifts waitressing and Freddie gigged across Barcelona in the evenings, making sure to get home to make love to me before I fell asleep.

Then we would spend the morning lying in bed, taking it in turns to cook breakfast for one another, or binging out on *Modern Family.*

One crazy morning, Fred and I had gotten talking about my Nana, who's totally against anything nontraditional – for example, we're talking from having sex before marriage, to having the teeniest tattoo imprinted on you. Fred had laughed cheekily and dared me, "Well, seeing as you've already failed on that first one with me, we might as well go all out with the second pet hate, right? Besides I am a rock star, and you're a rock star's girlfriend so…"

And so, hours later, we had both booked into a tattoo parlor to seal the deal.

We both had a small teardrop on the back of our necks; it was the one symbol that had in fact brought us closer and closer together.

Freddie's band, *The Rainer's*, is how we had first met, and on the second night we had met, Fred had held me in *Gatsby's*, tears running down my face. Freddie's Mum's name had also meant the warrior God of rain, and I respected her entirely for bringing up such a beautiful human.

Freddie said that no matter what happened, that tear, or raindrop, would bring back memories that one day we may well cry over, that may well be in sadness when we have to one-day part, or in happiness when telling others about our magical whirlwind romance.

As we exited the tattoo parlor I chuckled to myself, "Have fun explaining this bright idea to my Nana..." And he'd looked at me, that cheekiness evident in his eyes and said, "Well, hopefully she'll forgive me for this if I've married you by then."

I blushed, remembering how quickly my life had changed from being the reincarnation of Bridget Jones, listening to *All by Myself* and drowning myself in cheap wine and whisky.

~

It was at 4am when I got the call – Fred shot up beside me hearing the phone buzz to life. Noah's number flashed up. Oh gosh, had something happened to the kids? Or Iz? Or my parents? Nobody rings at that time in the morning just for a catchup.

"Hello, hello?" I questioned, sleepily yet slowly,

coming more and more alert with concern. My voice was hoarse.

"Hello Mam. This is DCI Groban calling. I have tried to contact your brother's wife, but I have had no

answer several times. This is just to let you know that your brother has been in a severe road collision, and is in critical condition."

I breathed in and found that I couldn't breathe out. Fred had hold of me with all of his body, rocking me as he heard the murmurs of the unwanted words... critical... collision... my big brother.

"How soon can you get to Queen Mary's?" DCI Groban asked, the concern suddenly becoming unconcealed.

"Hello? Miss? Are you there?"

"Y-y-y-ess I'm here," I said, my voice coated with shock and panic.

But the silence on the line was suddenly interrupted with the long, slow beep of a heart monitor and a paramedic screaming, "We're losing him! We're losing him!"

I jumped up out of bed and ran to grab my backpack, leaving Fred alone in the bedsheets we had made love in, just hours before.

"Baby I'm so sorry, I don't know what to do, let me

come with you, *please.*" Fred whispered as he climbed out of the bed, his eyes watery with sadness, his arm reaching out for me. But my barriers went up.

"I'm sorry Fred, I can't do this right now, I have to go. He's my brother. I'm so sorry."

Fred came over and tried to hug me but I pushed him away, "No! Please don't. Don't make this harder for me. I have to leave, now."

"Honey, let me come with you... Posy!!"

"No Fred. We knew this would come to an end, you have to leave to go and tour, we were just being immature and not thinking realistically. This is goodbye. Please, don't follow me. I don't want you to. Please." I whispered, sobbing into my hands.

"Babe, what are you saying?" he questioned, but I had no answer, my mouth was saying everything I didn't even mean to say, so I turned away.

"I have to go."

"Let me come with you, please. Baby, d-d-d-don't go!" He cried, the heartache causing his voice to break.

My only thoughts turned to my brother and though my heart ached to take Fred with me, I felt selfish and went with what my head said.

Noah was the priority.

I zipped my suitcase up and I fled the apartment, leaving Fred naked, innocent and lonely as ever.

The only thing I kept going over and over in my head was that the day Hamilton cheated on me, I lost my trust in love.

I know to take that out on Fred was completely out of order. But I did. And my heart ached every day because of it.

~

I fled the apartment and grabbed the nearest taxi, staring out of the fogged window as I drove away. In the blur of my eye, I saw Fred run out into the street and heard him scream out my name through the thin glass. A tear fell down my face. I wanted him so, so badly. But my brother was dying, he was dying and he was the only guy I needed to be thinking about.

The taxi drove through the cobbled streets of Barcelona, dashing past blurred memories and crawling across the haze of the early morning dew.

With my adrenaline kicking in, I checked my phone quickly and shouted "Vamos! Vamos!" to the driver, noting the next flight was just half an hour away.

We sped through the early morning traffic, taking the smaller, hidden routes and arriving with twenty minutes to spare. I ran to the front of the luggage queue, explaining my situation, and they pushed me to the front of each queue. Luckily my Spanish had improved a little since I first arrived and I could just about uphold a conversation.

Sitting down on the plane, it all hit me. The fact that my brother could or could not be dead, and that I wouldn't know for sure until I landed, or the fact that I had just ran away and broken the heart of the only guy I'd truly ever felt happy with. I wasn't sure which was worse.

Love and death are the greatest and most painful equalizer after all.

~

When I had landed back home after what felt like eternity, I got a taxi to the hospital and walked into a room where my brother lay battered and bruised, with two metal pads being pressed into his chest. As I was running along the white, cleansed yet painful corridors I heard a Nurse announcing that they'd lost him.

And I stopped running, my heart stopping too.

I couldn't move for the fear of collapsing, and having to accept that I was one step closer to the truth of losing my brother. Oh gosh, the kids. My beautiful niece and nephew, with no Daddy.

No. Please... No.

But with a shocking twist of fate and after forty minutes of being dead, my brother's heart miraculously started up again and I saw him burst back to life, his chest rapidly rising up and down.

As I had made my way in through the room, his heart monitor had started beeping again as he came back to life. I hope to think he knew I was there, and knew I needed him. That he wasn't allowed to leave me.

There was so much commotion in the tiny hospital room as I watched people in green and white help my brother to breathe painlessly. He remained unconscious and the doctors put him into an induced coma for the fear of him waking up and injuring his already damaged and broken spine.

I stayed by his bedside that night, alone. I had called Cousin Amy who was looking after Jessie and Niall to tell them that Daddy had been in a little accident, but that he was doing ok.

I switched into protective sister and Aunty mode... I didn't want to panic them too much. The poor little souls.

I'd also tried to contact Izzy and was disgusted that she didn't answer her phone after ten missed calls from me. Talk about a doctor being on call 24/7.

Izzy arrived hours later, saying that she had been on a late shift operating a last-minute heart transplant surgery, though I took note in the fact that she had had time to change from her scrubs into a pair of jeans and a blouse.

But I didn't have time to be angry as my love for

Noah prioritized my true emotions. Including my aching heart and desire to have Fred there, holding me, telling me it would all be okay. But I'd made the decision to walk out on him and break his heart.

Hamilton had arrived at the hospital hours after I had too, around the same time as Izzy had – he was the hospital's negligence lawyer, *unfortunately*.

The detectives explained the collision to him and Hamilton made notes, listening intently with his deep blue and deceivingly sweet eyes.

He kept glancing at me stood behind the glass partition looking into Noah's room. I felt utterly vulnerable and lonely with my brother in critical condition and I couldn't do one thing about it, nor could I have prevented it.

It's the domino effect. Other people's drunken choices had resulted in his broken, bruised and wounded body, and listening to the detective's description. the people in the other vehicle had walked away from the accident with as little as a scar.

Suddenly, Hamilton came over and hugged me, kissing me gently on the cheek. "I'm so sorry honey," he said lovingly, his memorable scent making me feel safe in his bear-hug arms.

He had this terribly annoying, controlling effect over me, when I was weak I would just fall back to him.

My hands shook uncontrollably as I let him hold me, appreciating the familiarity there between us.

He stared deeply into my eyes and kissed me passionately on my lips. Feeling vulnerable I let him.

That was until my brain waves kicked in and remembered his Dick personality, and I pushed him away.

"What the fuck are you doing?" I said, suddenly disgusted at myself for letting myself fall into that trap again, wiping my lips with the back of my hand. He looked shocked and turned beetroot red.

"Sorry Posy – I thought that…" He began.

"No, don't think anything."

We stood side by side in an awkward silence, an atmosphere you could have cut with a blunt knife.

A voice interrupted the awkward air settling between us, "Hammy man, have you managed to

collect all mobile phones off family members to confirm this wasn't a suicide attempt, et cetera?", a colleague shouted unprofessionally.

Hamilton nodded and turned around to me - already having read his mind - with my mobile phone in midair for him to collect.

"I'm sorry, it's procedure. I'll be as quick as I can okay?" He said sheepishly.

~

Noah surprised all of the doctors, but not his little sister when he opened his eyes for the first time in two months. He was yet to discover that the car crash had resulted in him temporarily losing function in both legs, and one arm, after having severe nerve damage in his back.

DCI Groban had described the collision for me in the early hours when I had hopped on a flight back home, leaving Fred begging for me to let him come home with me. But I told him not to. That my brother needed me. That my brother was the most important thing.

I regretted ever placing Freddie second best – he and Noah should have always been my equal firsts.

But we make mistakes, and sometimes make decisions that aren't really what our heart want, and that's why life is so beautifully and painfully complicated.

Then again, maybe if I hadn't have gotten on that plane my brother may have deteriorated alone, without even his wife to hold his hand.

And maybe, he wouldn't have recovered as well as he did if I hadn't had been by his bedside every day,

looking after the kids and Bob (the dog) with every moment I could spare – seeing as Iz went AWOL most of the time.

The crash had happened quickly and violently. Noah had been driving home after going to a school reunion, the kids at home being looked after by Cousin Amy.

Noah had been the designated driver, dropping off the drunken reunion friends off on his way home. Just as he was turning off the motorway, a group of drunken lads in a stolen car had come straight at him, driving the wrong way down the slip road and hit him head on.

Noah had done nothing. But he'd walked away with a lot more than that.

I had sat by his bedside day after day, he'd been in a coma for so long and the doctors were surprised when he was resuscitated successfully, never mind when he actually woke up and had some memory. My brother was a fighter for sure. Jessie and Niall brought their Daddy little gifts every day, even when he was in the coma, and they would read him their favourite stories. The hospital staff were kind enough to put up a bed for me in his room, and I stayed by him until I believed there was no chance of losing him.

Chapter 15

FREDDIE

Fate always decides, right?

After Posy had told me to not chase her, it had made me want to chase her even more. I had never fallen for anyone the way that I had fallen for Posy. She had taken me under her wing, listened to my past and talked about the future with me. I couldn't just let her become another song about letting go of something that I would one day regret.

I had grabbed the first change of clothes I could find and ran out of the door, hopping in the nearest taxi I could holler. I could not get the image of my Posy out of my head, and then her brother Noah, too. I had never met him but I knew him somehow.

Through Posy I felt her love for him and it utterly broke me.

Ironically, *"Holding Out for A Hero"* was blasting inside the cab when I climbed in. Talk about 'now's not the time'.

After racing to the airport, I had asked at the desk for the quickest flight back to Gatwick, but it wasn't until two hours later. I had missed Posy's flight by two minutes. I didn't know if it was just my imagination but I swore to myself that I had seen her in the distance at the check in. But I think it was just my heart playing games. She had gone.

Fuck.

I sat in the departures lounge watching everybody mindlessly looking through the shelves of duty free. My hands were fidgety as I sat helpless in a situation I so badly wanted to fix right there and then. My eyes pricked with tears.

After a very long two hours of waiting, the gate finally opened and I raced towards it.

Seated on the plane I turned numb. It was as if this huge weight had fallen onto my shoulders and my whole life was in the balance of one girl, and one plane ride to get to her.

The plane ride felt like eternity and I couldn't get comfy or even try to sleep with my mind racing.

Digging into my pocket I found an old scrap of paper and there was a pen in the foldaway tray compartment.

Songwriting was always the answer to every emotional situation:

Plane rides in the middle of the night,

Just want to see if you meant what you said,

When you said that I wasn't worth your time,

Because time is immeasurable, and love is impossible,

But we had something that was worth more than a dime.

I made the mistake of not saying a word when you walked out of the door,

Because baby I'm such a mess and I'm worth nothing anymore,

You were someone who listened to my late night small talk,

And brushed your cold feet against my legs to get warm,

On those hot nights, we lay in each other's arms,

And now, here we are.

Waiting to land in your homeland,

I need to see your face to know if you meant it,

When you said that I wasn't worth your time,

Because time isn't a crime, I mind spending with you,

Cos we had something that was as rare as sunshine,

on a cloudy afternoon.

I made the mistake of not saying a word when you slammed the taxi door,

Because baby I regret not trying to find a cure,

You were someone who listened to my late night small talk,

And said you liked my crooked teeth and my walk,

On those hot nights, we were dancing in the dark,

And now, here we are.

The biggest mistake I made was letting you fade away into the night,

Without putting up a fight,

Baby I hope he's alright,

Hope you'll be pleased to see me,

Tomorrow, first thing, in the early morning.

Whist on the plane, a gang of girls approached me - they all had *The Rainer's* t-shirts on and were all flushed red. They shyly asked for my autograph and so I complied happily. It kept my aching mind busy, and reminded me of the night I had first met Posy.

~

I reached the hospital a half hour after I landed, after hopping on a free shuttle that ran directly to it. I ran towards the reception area and inquired about Noah. After telling a very little yet purposeful white lie about being his step brother, I ran through the whitewashed halls to the ICU.

I wanted to be there for Posy. I wanted to be the one to tell her that everything was going to be alright. And that he'd make it through, because if he was anything like his sister, he'd be a real fighter.

Passing hospital rooms, I saw families laughing and lone elders crying into tissues as they watched the ones they loved fade away, and I saw the two extremes of love. The painful one that rips your heart in two, and the one that joins two hearts as one.

But then I saw them.

Hamilton and Posy kissing in the corridor outside

Noah's room. And my heart broke into a million pieces. I remembered Hamilton's face from the picture Posy had shown me.

In total shock, I walked out of the hospital, feeling selfish for intruding on an injured man all for the sake of winning back a girl who was in love with someone else.

As I walked out of the hospital doors, something inside me told me to try one more time. Some strange hope inside me told me that maybe it wasn't what I thought I'd seen.

And so, reaching in my pocket for my phone I rang Posy's number.

He picked up.

And I hung up.

I had my answer.

And it wasn't the one my heart had wanted. I walked away, and this time I didn't run after her.

Pushing my way back out of the hospital, my heart sunk to the deepest depths and all I could think of was if Mum was here I would just cry into her arms.

I thought that my high school heartbreaks were

bad, but Posy not wanting me anymore was a deeper kind of pain.

One that made my hands screw up into tight fists,

and my eyes pulse with teary sadness.

I stayed in Kent for a few days, but I didn't hear from Posy. I had to tell myself that it was over, and that it really was what it looked like – a whirlwind romance.

Chapter 16

POSY

Dreaming with a broken heart

So, remember me telling you about my venture to
Austria on my travels? Well surprisingly I came
across another guy who claimed to not be a
knobhead and ended up being 100% a knobhead.
He was the Daniel Cleaver of Austria (Bridget Jones
fans will know what I mean). He was charming and
undeniably an arsehole, and he played me like a
game of Junior Monopoly. And I'm not so fucking
good at Monopoly.

I first saw Alfie Dalton outside of Schönbrunn
Palace. He was a teacher stood amongst a group of
students having a picture taken and I was simply
endlessly gazing at the Baroque detail on the
palace.

It was my day off as I worked just a few days a week teaching English at the local Volksschule. I remember him first looking at me just as I was trying to discreetly pull my knickers out of my arse crack - last time I wore a silk thong I'll tell you. Silk has nothing to bloody cling onto. Nada.

I kept bumping into Alfie throughout the afternoon. I kept making sure to stand behind him and pretend to gaze at the palace, when in reality I was gazing at the pure plumpness of his beautifully crafted arse.

He had sandy blonde Justin Bieber-ish hair, tortoise shell glasses, a grey hoodie and worn out white trainers on. He had really nice hands, sculpted by angels and he kept enthusiastically moving them about when explaining the architecture to the students. I was mesmerized - you cannot go wrong with a guy with nice hands. Or at least that's what I had always told myself.

I kept trying to work up the courage to go over and speak to him, but I feared that rejection in front of his entire class could be a push over the edge for poor Posy. And besides, every other girl there was staring at him too. So, I just kept doing what most girls would do which was to keep flicking my hair and hoping he'd have more courage than me.

We had a pretty infamous meet cue because I accidentally walked into the men's toilets and saw more than I needed to see of Alfie. His first words to me were, "You can't come in here unless you have a penis. And I really hope you don't, because you're outstandingly beautiful, and we should go out sometime."

Sometimes I think back and wonder if he would have ever spoken to me if it wasn't for my clumsiness that day. It would have saved me a whole lot of heartbreak. And it would have been one less notch in his belt.

Anyway, I fell for him. Hard. Harder than I should have.

I wish I'd have known sooner that I'd never be the person at the top of his list.

He was the type of guy that preferred to be perfectly lonely than to give me everything. I had already written the story of us in my head before it had even begun.

And yet, somewhere deep inside me I knew we would never be a bestseller. I just went all Taylor Swift on you then, didn't I?

After exchanging phone numbers and lesson plans (AKA late night teacher banter), we met up a few days later.

We went to a chilled little bar where a local tribute

band were playing. We both sat talking for hours, our first connection was our ability to sing every word to every single John Mayer song.

We had our first kiss that night. I stupidly never thought we'd have a last kiss.

He was a really busy guy, he taught art history full time throughout the day and was in a jazz band by night. He was mesmerizing; we would talk for hours and he made me feel like I couldn't live without him. Our dates were so much fun, and neither of us wanted them to end - we went trampolining, we hiked up Kufstein and he even took me to the Salzburg festival. He did it all right.

We met up six or seven more times before he invited me back to his city apartment. We made love against his piano and then moved into his bed. He was so gentle with me, perfectly touching every part of me almost as if it was too good to be true. He kissed me slowly and used his fingers to make my spine curve with pleasure. I placed myself on top of him, after our first time together. His head rested in the crevice of my neck, both in awe of how alive we could make each other feel, my hair tickling his shoulder. We ended up just kissing for hours. Every kiss of his lingered on my neck like footprints in the sand.

He was so romantic too. After we had both climaxed he would keep hold of me and just run his fingers along my stomach, drawing circles around my tummy and then along my backbone. He would say "You're addictive. I never want it to stop when we're together. You do something to me Posy. You're beautiful, you know that right?"

Sex with Hamilton was always just 'meh'. It was usually because he was in the totally wrong spot. He couldn't tell pelvis from clitoris. And then it would take him that long to arouse me that my leg would start cramping up. Everyone deserves orgasms, so don't settle for someone you've got to fake it with or end up getting dead arse with because he's taking that long to 'release' himself. And you're just moaning loudly so he'll get on with it and get off you.

The moral of my little rant is if the sex is good, he's a keeper. Hamilton was never too gifted in that area. Alfie made me realize this about Hamilton because he knew exactly where I needed everything, and when to do it.

But Alfie wasn't just romantic, he could also be cheeky too and I liked that.

Sometimes I would meet him on his lunch break from school and we would sneak back to his apartment.

His piano keys spent a lot of time with my arse on them - they were comfier than you might think actually. That was until he was thrusting passionately this one time and then 'the moment' was ruined because we were both in hysterics as my arse had somehow managed to master *Phantom of the Opera* on the piano keys.

Jodie had always warned me about dating teachers because they often love their lesson plans more than you. And she had also warned me about dating musicians because they often preferred to write songs about you than to actually spend time with you. So, I should have known. And in a way, I guess I did know but I wanted to not know. You know?

He was like a drug.

I wanted him running through my veins because he made me feel good, if only for a moment. And despite not hearing from him for days at times, I kept reissuing him chances. Chances that he quite honestly didn't deserve. But he had a hold on me. I got lost in his soft lips and his hands. Those hands.

And then he stopped calling.

I tried getting in touch with him several times, but I got nothing. I was completely and utterly heartbroken by this guy I barely knew.

He didn't want me for life, I was just a convenient rental that fitted into his travelling schedule. I thought I knew him, but I guess all that we ever know is what people choose to show us.

I turned into one of those apartment hermits. I just didn't leave my room.

The truth is, I think he got scared because we had something so alive, so treasurable. And he ran away like a little boy. The difference is, he didn't come running back like a grown up man would have.

The one that ran away, if you will.

~

I ran into him a few weeks after the silent treatment. By this time, I was back on my feet, still heartbroken, but back in the world of the living.

It was a Saturday, and he and his band were performing at a wedding that I also happened to be waitressing at. Austria is expensive as hell and I took on any job that I could, so that I didn't end up using leaves to wipe my bum.

I remember seeing him on stage as I was carrying over the celebration cake, knife in hand - I froze in my tracks like an ice queen.

He spotted me straight away and I think he pretty much shit his pants. My face was set in pure 'resting bitch face' and it said, "If you dare approach me, I'll use this knife in my hand to detach something from you."

And so, *I* approached *him*, because I needed to say something. He started babbling on, turning redder by the second, and blaming his disappearance on his music. I didn't say anything until he shut up... finally. Ironically *"Talk Too Much"* by COIN was playing over the speakers.

"The only reason I came over here is to give you a bottle of grow the fuck up!" I shouted above the music.

I stood on the stage and poured a bottle of vodka over his musical equipment; seeing it frazzle and smoke was so satisfying. He then exclaimed, "Oh my fucking god! My music!!"

I shouted back, "Oh yeah, thought that might be the thing you run after you giant fuckwank!"

I lost my job that night for my use of fuck and wank in the same sentence. On the plus side, Alfie lost his pride and I gained mine back.

Posy 1. Alfie 0.

I didn't want him under my skin ever again no matter how good it had felt. Though he'd made me a stronger person, he'd only ever given me half of his heart. That's never a good sign.

The only thing he wore on his sleeve was his tattoo, and to be truthful his heart was nowhere to be seen.

I would spend nights endlessly staring at my phone, hoping his name would pop up. Silence is the worst heartbreaker when all you want is to hear their voice. It's something I've never been able to get my head around - the idea that some guys only ever want you when you're already two feet out of the door. They'll only chase you when they realize what they could have had. And that's your cue to go and pour a bottle of vodka on something that they love more than you. Or drink one. Either one works.

~

Unfortunately, like a drug I went back to Alfie. Just for one more hit.

It was almost like closure, because the next morning I caught my flight to Barcelona and never thought about him again. I shouldn't have done it because he didn't deserve one last night with me, but I needed him inside me one last time, because I really did love him in some strange and unhealthy way.

I feel like I should apologize because I shouldn't have gone back to someone who didn't deserve me, but I did and I can't explain why.

We all have that one person that we can't explain why we went back to them, even though they broke us. I guess, in a way, it's human nature.

Chapter 17

POSY

I couldn't make it up

I remember the evening vividly in my mind, like a nightmare you couldn't sleep over – it just never went away, no matter how hard I tried to block it out.

Two long years ago, Hamilton and I had been out for a lovely meal in London, a romantic lunch – something very rare in our relationship. We'd then returned home and had the normal, usual sex that was over within twenty minutes, and satisfied only him – but something wasn't quite right. He seemed like he was waiting for something... he was acting odd.

And every woman who's ever been cheated on can

feel when something isn't right, in more ways than one.

~

I'd had my suspicions over the year – Hamilton had always been the guy that every girl wanted, and he had cheated on me once in our teens (remember Cressida Jeems?). One flaw of mine is that I easily forgive the flaws of others; it's a weakness he knew I had, and he tried to use it against me.

I'd found various knickers hanging around the house over the years, or lurking in the bedroom drawers, and every time I asked him he'd simply say, "Oh, maybe they're Jodie's from when she stayed over? Or yours – you probably don't remember because you've got that bloody many!" He must have been keeping them as souvenirs. Dirty pervert. He was charming and persuasive. He fooled me.

~

After Hamilton and I had finished our usual routine following our romantic lunch, I showered and got ready to go out for girl's night with Jodie – which was usually one Friday a month.

Sometimes we were spontaneous and would spend an evening playing the penny flip game; you pick a number and either heads or tails, and that then determines where your destination will be.

At every turn you flip the coin, heads means left and tails right.

And whichever number you choose determines how long you will travel in that direction. But sometimes we were simply too tired to venture all the way out, and went for a lazy cinema chick-flick outing. That night, we had chosen to do the latter.

As I was heading out of the door - it must have been about 5pm by then - Hamilton came to tell me that he'd be heading to bed early, as he had a big court case in the morning, one that could potentially determine if he got tenure. He had kissed me goodbye and I went on my merry way, my arm linked with Jodie's, off to watch a film with Matthew Mccona-WAHEY in. AKA: Phwoar!!

Jodie and I chatted and giggled on our way to the cinema, about her non-existent love life and the frank lack of satisfying sex in both of our lives. Since we were kiddies I had desperately been trying to set Jodie up with my brother, Noah, but she always said he just wasn't her type. And so, Noah got brokenhearted and found Izzy, his wife, one drunken night at uni – how time flies.

When we got to the cinema we queued up for our tickets because the collection machines were broken. What made the situation even worse was that Jodie had accidentally clicked the wrong option and booked us two senior tickets, instead of adult tickets and so we had to stand explaining to the cashier why we didn't have boobs down to our kneecaps, or teeth that fell out if we laughed too hard.

But eventually, after a discussion with the manager over how next time we should 'learn to book the tickets *properly'*, we entered Screen 6 and sat waiting for the trailers.

Jodie and I were the stingy type of people, you know, the type who carry contraband into the cinema – I mean, c'mon, who pays £5 for a crappy, little box of popcorn when you can get two bags for £1.60 in posho Waitrose?

As the lights started dimming, people were still filtering in through the doors, attempting to find their seat numbers with their phone flashlights. Jodie and I always played this game where we would guess who would be sat next to us. Most of the time, though we dreamed about having this hunky, single guy next to us, it was usually some middle aged wrinkly not particularly there just for the film... Though that night was different – you just couldn't make it up.

It was nearly completely dark as the trailers came to an end and everyone in the cinema hushed, all that was to be heard was the loud, inconsiderate popcorn crunchers.

As the film started, a giggly girl who'd had a couple of Jager bombs, considering the state of her breath, asked to get past us. And gripping on to Stinky Breath's arse cheeks pushing her along our row was no one other than… Hamilton.

My mouth dropped open – what the actual fuck?

My husband was in the same cinema screening as me, cheating on me right before my very eyes, and I just didn't know what to say. I couldn't move. And not only were they on the same row, but out of all of the seats in the cinema, they were directly next to us. Jodie's breathing had gotten faster and I could hear the top of her kettle was about to go toooooooooooooooooooooootttttttt!

Jodie, a surge of anger suddenly raging through her veins, and doing her best friend duty for me, stood up in the middle of the cinema and screamed to Hamilton "You, my friend are a FUCKING TWAT! Do you all hear that? This guy right here is cheating on his wife with this dimwit who frankly is in the wrong Screen. Fucking 'Frozen' is that way babe." Jodie pointed and then turned her attention to Stink Breath and said, "I think PG is more your scene… And you've got your parent with you I can see?"

Noticing that I had frozen, Jodie grabbed my hand softly and said, "C'mon let's get you out of here."

Walking out of the screen was and still is a blur to this day. Jodie practically held me up as I both loved and hated Hamilton in the most incomprehensible way possible.

As we walked through the quiet streets of Kent, I sobbed into Jodie's shoulder, none of us needing to utter a word.

Jodie systematically rang Noah and asked him to meet us back at my place... she said it was urgent.

When we arrived back, Noah was already inside the house, the kettle boiling away. He knew me too well.

Jodie passed me over to Noah like a fragile newborn, and he held me up with his arms, kissing the top of my head gently and rubbing my back in soothing rhythms.

"Tell me everything when you're ready." Noah soothed.

~

Jodie ended up filling him in on the unbelievable (but predictable) series of events. It was the most explicit monologue I have ever witnessed.

"Are you fucking kidding me? He's cheating on you... again? The bastard. Posy, what screen were you in? I'm gonna go in there and that guy is gonna leave without his knob attached!" Noah shouted.

"No, you're not," I uttered, the first words I had managed to get out all evening.

"I don't love him anymore," I continued. "In fact, I

hate him. I don't want him... I don't want him anymore."

Jodie stared at me in shock. "How are you being so calm about this honey?"

Jodie and Noah were sat either side of me, listening to every word I spoke as I told them about the times he had come home smelling of sweet, cheap perfume or the knickers that kept turning up in various places.

"The truth is; I've known it all along. But he persuaded me that they were mine, or yours Jodie from when you stay over. But I've gotten so used to living in this safe haven I call home that I didn't want to tell anyone about my suspicions. I feel like I'm always paranoid because of what he did when we were younger, but now I know." I whispered, my voice as quiet as a mouse, speaking volumes.

"But honey, why didn't you tell us?" Noah asked, genuinely concerned.

"Because... because, I know you've got a lot on with Jessie and Niall, and Jodie has so much stress at work. It was just a crazy suspicion of mine, and I didn't want to open up a can of worms and ruin what I thought was a marriage I wanted to remain in."

Still, they looked at me, transfixed at my numbness.

I laughed out loud all of a sudden and Jodie and Noah both looked at one another, both seemingly confused at my abrupt mood change.

"I can't believe you told that girl that she could only watch PG films!" I giggled uncontrollably, placing my head in my hands in disbelief.

And as Jodie recalled the story to Noah, we all sat sipping cups of teas and chuckling, somewhat unaware of what the next day held.

~

The next morning, there was an abrupt knock at the door, I knew the knock rather well as this particular knob lost his key every week.

I never thought anything of it at the time, Hamilton was generally just irresponsible with anything he possessed. He was probably losing his keys because he kept leaving his pants with every girl he slept with.

Jodie and Noah were sandwiching me as we had all fallen asleep on the sofa, lifeless from the events the night before. It's strange how calm I felt – sure I was angry, but it was almost as if this euphoric wave had come along and knocked me over, bringing me back to the reality that I'd never been happily married to Hamilton.

Sure, he'd won me over with false happiness, buying me an Audi for my 21st birthday, buying me jewellery (the boutique kind, not the Argos kind), and wooing me with various trips to posh hotels in London. But it was all false happiness, it wasn't what I actually wanted. I wanted a guy that would come home and watch a movie with me on a Friday night, or take me camping in a secluded muddy field, or even take a road trip with me in an old Corvette. Money gave Hamilton this hold over me, but it was a false type of happiness, the kind of happiness that you imitate when you see someone you really don't like, but have to pretend you do. We've all got them in the family haven't we…

After so many years of marriage, and a cheating husband I was sincerely calmer than a person on Kalms. With Noah and Jodie still fast asleep, I made my way to the door.

I opened the door to a guy that looked as if he'd been dragged through a hedge backwards, and then been sprayed by a skunk. I said nothing and let him speak first.

"Babykins I'm sorry. Nothing happened I promise. I made a mistake… I was stupid to do that to you. I promise it will never happen again."

And do you know what I did in reply? I laughed. I laughed for a good ten minutes at his pathetic attempt to win me over, especially after he smelt of sex and he'd been missing the entire night.

I shut the door leaving him speechless and

confused at my giggling hyena impression. I walked into the kitchen, grabbed my Audi A1 car keys, then ran upstairs and grabbed my jewellery box, feeling calm yet sassy. A new woman. Taking my time walking back down the stairs, wanting to make his pain and suspicion last as long as I possibly could, I opened the door.

"You can have this, and this, and this Hamilton, because quite frankly it never made me happy." I calmly told him, whilst throwing each item with quite some force where I knew it would hurt.

"But, I-I-I..." Hamilton began, protecting his crotch area.

I cut him off, "But you, what? C'mon, spit it out?"

He was silent and as a red as a beetroot. Ha! Hamilton never got embarrassed, so for me this was quite the achievement!

"C'mon, let me show you how much I love you, let's go upstairs?" He pleaded, trying to force his hands onto my breasts.

"No. What the hell? Are you actually having a laugh, Hamilton? My vibrator pleasures me more than you, so that's a no," I said, pushing his hand away.

"Next week, you can also have the house back," I continued. "I will be leaving you as of next Friday, and until then I don't want to see you. In fact, the next time I see you will be in court okay, *darling*?"

I added the darling on for extra pedantic effect. Go me!

I finished our conversation with a door slam just to twist his balls that extra bit further.

I walked back into the kitchen, sassy as ever, like one of those car chase films where you imagine explosions going off behind the heroic driver, and opened the baking cupboard.

I was in fact walking away from a burning vehicle right there and then, and next time I wanted a reliable car, not some naff five door estate like Hamilton.

Grabbing the flour, flaxseed and blueberries, I cooked up a batch of vegan blueberry pancakes - Jodie had introduced me to the recipe a while back and I fell in love with it, from day one. One might say it's better than sex – well better than sex with Hamilton anyway... BURNNNN!

I then flicked on the radio and "Wake Up Boo" came blasting out of the speakers. I jumped around crazily and let the music travel through my veins. I could still see his figure standing outside of the window and so stood in front of it like a lunatic dancing like I was on more than paracetamol. I think he always had a suspicion that I had an extra dose of crazy than the average person. But if he didn't like that, so be it. I did. And someone else would someday too.

Chapter 18

POSY

My little Rugrats

I remember the night pretty vividly. I was sat with Hamilton binge watching and (secretly) ogling Liev Schreiber in reruns of *Ray Donovan,* when my phone buzzed to life. It was Noah.

"You're officially an Aunty," he whispered down the phone, "Get your butt down to the hospital to meet my son."

I had literally cried down the phone and not even bothered to change out of my flannel, pink-fleece pajamas to go to the hospital. I was out of the car before Hamilton had even parked, and I ran so fast into the ward where my sweet little nephew was waiting. When Noah and Izzy had found out that they were pregnant I was so upset, knowing that deep down I wanted children, but I had a womb and husband who didn't.

Then I'd thought rationally about the fact that maybe being an Aunty was my destiny.

As I walked into the whitewashed hospital room that brought back painful and cancerous childhood memories, I saw a tiny blue bundle in the arms of my brother. I remember Noah looking so old, so mature. It felt like five minutes since we were little rugrats running wild on The Island with Dad, and Noah standing there with his own son suddenly put it all into perspective.

Izzy even cracked a smile at me when Noah passed over little Niall into my arms. He smelt like a baby and I couldn't stop kissing him over and over again. Noah took endless pictures and after about thirty minutes Hamilton finally found the room, claiming he'd gotten lost when in actual fact I knew he was chatting up the short-skirted midwife on Ward 9. I'd clocked her on the way in. His typical type. Replica of Cressida Jeems.

~

I watched Niall grow up and blossom. I heard him say his first word, I gift wrapped his wobbly teeth when they fell out and told him magical stories about the tooth fairy. I even bought him his first balance bike.

Izzy, on the other hand, was pretty much out of the picture. She'd suffered with postnatal depression and totally rejected Noah and Niall for a good year.

She took sick leave from work for the year and after a lot of therapy returned the year after, making her patients a greater concern than her family.

When Niall had sticky fingers I would wipe them, or if he had a nightmare and his Dad was asleep, he would sit under his cover and ring me on the house phone, and I would talk for hours to him on the phone, until he fell back asleep.

Then little Jessie had come along as a surprise. Izzy hadn't realized that she was pregnant until she was six months in, and though Noah and I were worried about Izzy's mental state in having another child, she ensured us that she would be okay. And so, one very snowy Christmas Eve many years ago, Izzy had popped for a bath and out popped Jessie. She'd delivered the baby herself with her doctorate knowledge, and a healthy 6lb little girl had literally plopped into the world.

Why is it that some women can literally just pop a baby out? I mean, I know for a fact that if it were me it would be like a murderous, sweaty labyrinth down there and last for two days straight. I'm not graceful in any respect, so giving birth would definitely not be a pretty sight.

~

After many years of looking after Niall and Jessie and taking them to various theme parks in between my part time teaching job, I began thinking a lot.

I realized how I really wanted a baby. I noticed how maternal I was and how non-fraternal Hamilton was – for example, his idea of a kid's day out was taking them into his office to organize some shelves, and do a bit of colouring on the back of some scrap paper from the fax machine.

The only problem was that I had gotten so comfortable in my life and being married to him that I didn't dare say a word. I didn't want to lose him. I was always so jealous of other women saying how they would kill for a guy like Hamilton, and so I put my own happiness onto the side plate, and kept Hamilton's feelings on the main course menu.

I often thought of how painful it would be to lose him, but I'm unsure if that was really the pain of knowing I'd truly be better off if I found someone that cared more about me, than themselves.

Chapter 19

POSY

The moment he knew

I had always had suspicions about Izzy since the day she'd married my brother one winter's dawn. Sure, she was beautiful, lovely and kind of liked by everyone in the family (except me), but she had this unhealthy hold over my brother. She was so controlling, and I could see Noah falling for her, but he seemed so happy, so I kept my big mouth shut.

He and Izzy had met on a drunken night out at uni, and within a few weeks she had moved into his little dingy flat in Kent, overtaking his usually basic décor with ounces of pink and yellow, and volumes of Floral Febreze.

Iz had never really taken to me after I had shown up drunk one night (which was rare, I promise), after forgetting my key to my apartment – and Hamilton was no help because he was off on a post-exam all-weeker in Kos.

Noah had made me a bed up on their sofa very kindly, and tucked me up with a glass of orange juice and few aspirin, in preparation for a very painful morning.

It was Jodie's fault I had gotten drunk – she was always my, "C'mon you could die tomorrow, and wouldn't you regret not having that last tequila shot?" kind of friend.

We had partied all night and gotten kicked out of various bars for our drunkenness. A night to remember, and one I haven't re-lived since. Me and sickness do not go well together – I'm crabby and miserable and I don't like not being able to eat. Food is too good.

Izzy had this false, hair-flicky, glossy-lipped persona that she put on around everyone but me. She loved my Mum and adored Dad, but totally disapproved of me. Sure, I was a little bit crazy and eccentric, but in a good way. I wore flowers in my hair and spoke with *some* expletives, but I wasn't the hardest person to get along with. As I was falling asleep on their sofa that was way too small for my long, spindly Daddy long legs, I had overheard Noah and Iz talking in their bedroom.

"She's an absolute disaster Noah. She's bringing

absolute disgrace to the family, and quite frankly she needs to sort her booze problem out."

"Her booze problem?" He had replied calmly, knowing full well I was the type of person who had one glass of wine every Monday, and the occasional beer on a Sunday evening.

She'd gone off on a tangent about alcohol poisoning, dropping in all of her medical knowledge, and Noah didn't say a thing for a while – she's a difficult person to interrupt, mind you. Voice like a fucking humpback whale.

Noah had concluded the argument with, "Look, I understand you care about her but she's fine... honestly."

And from that moment on she had looked at me and treated me as if I was a piece of dog shit on her Louboutin shoe. She 'forgot' to invite me to her hen night following her and Noah's engagement, and she made up various excuses to not come out on 'bonding' trips with me.

That, however, probably had something to do with my type of shopping involving charity shops and her type of shopping involving going down those high streets that I usually avoided, for fear of looking homeless amongst the rich.

Their wedding had cost about £50,000 – Izzy's parents were rich and mine were over generous, in particular my Mother. They'd gotten hitched at an all-inclusive gold-platinum resort, with all the trimmings and a six-foot-tall cake. Izzy's dress had been made by some designer I can't pronounce, nor spell.

The dress had a long trail which stretched about eighteen feet long. I know you're going to totally disapprove of my behavior but at the wedding, Izzy had tripped over her veil as she was walking down the aisle, and I had burst out laughing - like crying-on-the-verge-of-weeing laughing. Even Noah and Hamilton had cracked a smile, but she'd given me absolute evils. Oh, what a blushing bride she was. She was the Regina George and I was the Gretchen.

My bridesmaid speech was also sincerely painful, I had to bullshit on about how wonderful Izzy was, and how lucky Noah was to be marrying a dear friend of mine. It's a good job I'm a good liar when I need to be, because I had a whole other speech planned if she decided to show any traits of her usual behavior. My other speech began with, "So this fucking bitch..."

But what can you do if you don't like the woman that your brother loves? Essentially, nothing. It was out of my hands.

I just wish I had told him about my real feelings earlier.

~

Prior to Noah's car accident, Izzy had been working overtime a lot, and sure, she was a doctor, it does require a lot of your time. But it was happening more and more frequently, and ironically during periods where Noah and the kids had planned to go away, almost as if she had better things to do.

It was the evening of the crash when I realized that she was having an affair.

She had shown up that dreadful evening, late and not because of traffic, claiming she'd come directly from an emergency heart surgery but was dressed in stilettos, jeans, a blouse and stunk of *Hugo Boss for Men*. Now unless she was planning on becoming transgender sometime in the near future, there was no other explanation for her aftershave overload.

But Noah needed me and so I left her to it; my brother was my main priority.

Fred was always lingering at the back of my mind, like some painful memory that I wanted so badly to erase, yet so desperately wanted to grip onto until my knuckles turned white.

I hoped one day our past would find us again but dreaded that I had blown it.

One day - a few weeks after Noah's accident, when Jessie and Niall's school rang me asking why no one had picked them up from after school club - I finally confronted Izzy.

After going to pick up the kids and bring them back to the hospital to sit with their Daddy for a little while, I grabbed my coat and headed to Noah and Izzy's house along Whitehill.

I was fucking fuming.

Driving up I saw a car I recognized outside the house – an Audi A1. It was black. Oh no it couldn't be. SHUT the front door.

I stormed across the street and into the house after abandoning my car. Then I slammed the front door behind me to try and make Izzy aware that I was entering the house, just in case anyone was entering her!

As I came to the bottom of the staircase, I saw a familiar figure.

Hamilton walked out onto the landing wearing absolutely nothing, his dick wavering like a swinging watch, as he saw me standing at the bottom of the stairs.

You must be fucking kidding. What the fuckety fuck fuck.

"What the FUCK are you doing here you dick?" I said, not really asking him for a reply, my tone of voice threatening that if he dared answer back, his swing watch of a cock would no longer be attached.

He froze as Izzy shouted from the bedroom "Baby,

why don't you come and do that special thing I like to my wet little hole, I've still got half an hour before I have to go to the hospital."

Oh, good god I thought. *Let me just vomit in my mouth. That is fucking disgusting.*

After recovering from nearly vomiting my entire stomach contents onto the cream carpet, I stormed up the stairs as Hamilton held onto his very small amount of manhood with his hairy hands.

"Thank you for putting your knob away, it was never a pretty fucking sight!" I shouted at him, before storming into the bedroom, raring to go.

"You fucking heartless fucking bitch!" I exploded as I walked in to see Izzy handcuffed to the bedpost.

Classy.

I suddenly felt myself turning into Jodie with the amount of 'fucks' coming out of my mouth.

"Your husband is lying in a hospital bed with your beautiful children whom *I* have just been to pick up from school. And *you* are here fucking your brains

out with this fucking excuse of a man that used to be my husband? You have some serious problems Izzy considering you're a fucking doctor. Don't they usually know when people need to get FUCKING help?"

She had stared at me, shock evident on her face, unable to move from the restraints on her wrists.

I kept looking to and fro between Hamilton and Izzy, in pure disgust at the fact that they were both starkers *and* cheating excuses of spouses.

"Don't be expecting me to brush over it like this is just an innocent fuck because your husband's 'out of action'. You have kids, two beautiful ones that need you right now."

I walked over to the bedside before leaving, and shouted, "Oh and put your fucking Bridget Jones knickers on please, because frankly you need a trim down there, it looks like the fucking Amazon Jungle Izzy!"

Then, turning towards my ex-husband I pedantically said, "And Hamilton, I'd try and get a doctor's appointment soon because you seem to have a little infection going on down there, and possibly a shrinkage issue."

His eyes darted from me down to his dangly knob, and I was thankful Fred's hadn't looked anything like his wrinkly, little todger.

I walked out of there, angry inside, yet rather pleased with the fact that Hamilton was that desperate in life to sleep with his own sister in law.

And I felt empowered somehow, yet desperately sorry for Noah's future. It wouldn't be easy, but without *her* around it would certainly be a lot happier. You've got to outrun the cheaters and leave them, and their trails, far behind.

I couldn't believe the fucking situation I'd just walked in on, and swiftly out of.

If little knobs were her thing and if hairy bushes were his, they could both please one another as far as I was concerned.

She wouldn't be going anywhere near my brother again, and Hamilton wouldn't be touching me even if it was with a barge pole.

Izzy was frankly never working overtime, unless that was Hamilton's new nickname.

~

A couple of days later, I was sat explaining *it* all to Jodie.

Then I remembered Jodie telling me months before about her hearing Hamilton talking to someone called Belle at the supermarket... Belle... Izabelle... Izzy!!!

I decided not to say a word to my brother, because quite frankly it wasn't my place to say it. Izzy was the one who had done the dirty, and I wasn't about to fulfill a deed that was her duty to her husband.

I felt so helpless, knowing my brother had already

been through hell, to then be greeted by his devil of a wife. It killed me to the core. Yet I wanted it to just be said so that we could all move on from pretending.

~

One day I was sat outside Noah's room - forcing myself to drink a cup of tea that one of the nurses had kindly made for me, but she had oversqueezed the teabag so that I was left with tea leaves stuck in between my teeth - when Izzy came confidently striding down the corridor and headed straight inside. What I'd like to call the snooty bitch walk.

I heard the entire conversation between them, and it was a lot less eventful and dramatic than I'd anticipated. It was concluded with Noah telling Izzy to "Go Fuck herself."

I have to admit; I was pretty proud of my brother for borrowing one of my famous sayings.

Izzy walked out a little less confidently, and a tad bit more sheepishly. That's right, she had her tail between her legs, and by tail I don't mean Hamilton's tail. If it could even pass as a tail that is. More along the size of a baby carrot.

There's a reason I rarely orgasmed with him when we were married - baby carrots don't reach to the places they need to.

I had walked straight into Noah's hospital room as

Izzy had stormed out. I ran straight over to hug my brother.

"I knew." He confessed.

I sat gob smacked as he told me about he knew Izzy had been having an affair because she had called him a different name in bed on numerous occasions.

And he said that her shifts just didn't add up, that she was constantly dubious.

But do you know what his main concern was? Whether I was okay because it was Hamilton she'd been sleeping with.

I'd laughed out loud at his concern and replied, "Honey, I'm a little too old and a little more experienced to know when I should get off the ride these days. Let's just hope they don't go and have a baby together, because that would be one FUCKING dickhead of a child."

He'd asked me about Barcelona and I brushed over how important Fred really was to me, because truth be told, every time I let myself think about him – even if just for a second – my heart ached.

I'd fallen for a guy who I'd only known for a few weeks, and I couldn't understand why I couldn't just move on. Maybe it was because it was me who had done the heartbreaking, almost as if I couldn't let myself heal.

The reality was the one guy I had walked out on was the one guy I'd ever regretted letting go of. The only guy who knew *me* for me, and the only man I'd ever truly loved with every last aching part of my heart. Shitballs indeed.

Chapter 20

NOAH

The unexpected

Before Izzy had officially confessed to her numerous affairs, one of them being with my sister's ex-husband, I hadn't really ever thought that I could fall in love with someone else.

But I did. And it happened within a matter of a week.

I guess I had been ignoring the fact that the spark had fizzled out with me and Izzy years ago, but still, I didn't go and sleep with someone else, so I guess she gets a red card for that move. She screwed up what started off as a masterpiece. I should have ended it when she said that my sister was a waste of space, but my heart blurred my decision-making skills.

After my car accident, I was referred to a memory clinic specialist as some of my short memory had been lost in the accident. It wasn't drastic, but sometimes I noticed myself asking silly questions twice, instead of once, or walking out of a room and forgetting why I had even gotten out of bed. But it wasn't just regular forgetfulness, it was a little bit more extreme, and it made my brain hurt if I thought too hard.

My memory therapist was called Nancy and she had my attention in an instant. She had black hair straight down to her belly button, and piercing auburn eyes, with plumped peachy lips that spoke words that I listened too, but didn't really take in. She was mesmerizing.

The first thing that she mentioned was that she had only been told about my injuries from the accident. All other details of others that were involved (meaning the drunken wanker that had hit me head on) were classed as confidential initially, unless I gave her permission to involve them in our sessions. I trusted her within an instant, and seemed to almost cling onto the idea of her, knowing that my wife was long gone.

Nancy had introduced herself as "Dr Nancy Crafton, but you can call me Nancy if you like."

The doctors had mentioned that whilst my back was still healing I would have some problems getting a… you know… but as soon as I saw Dr Nancy Crafton twiddling her pen between her fingers, I had to awkwardly squish down a very big erection. How embarrassing. A grown man with no control over himself. It reminded me of the days in high school when you had a teacher who was super-hot teaching you sex education. The joys of puberty. Though, there was a guy in our year who suffered really bad with control over his… urges. He was nicknamed Bret Boner. Initially, it was a name that he hated being called, but when he got into sixth form he was a big hit with the ladies! Ha-ha!

Luckily Nancy hadn't noticed my erection, or at least if she had she had been very discreet about it.

The first words I had blurted out to her were, "You're very pretty Nancy." I was so embarrassed. I was like a boy talking to a girl he liked for the first time.

Nancy had blushed as I had apologized for my bluntness. She thanked me for my honest compliment, and said she hadn't heard that for a long time.

We spoke about a lot of things, about my childhood, about the accident and also about Posy a lot. I told Nancy that there was someone Posy really liked but she wouldn't go and chase after them. I said I felt it was my stupid bloody fault for going and getting myself nearly killed, and Nancy had listened intently.

"You certainly care about your sister, don't you Noah?" Nancy had inquired in her hushing tone, "Caring about someone is good for the memory. Love somehow makes a lot of forgettable things unforgettable. Like for example, seeing a blue pebble amongst a heap of beige shells on a beach one day might be forgettable to some, but if you have the person you love beside you, it may well be a memory you remember and recall until the day you die."

Nancy and I saw one another twice a day, and by 'saw' I mean for an appointment unfortunately, not a romantic, candlelit dinner date. Sigh.

Nancy also happened to have a lot of dog training experience, and so helped the kids and I to teach Bob a few tricks that could come in handy in helping me with my newly acquired faulty left arm.

Bob became a pretty helpful source in the hospital room. I don't think you realize how handy the 'Retrieve' command is until you drop your boxers, so you're left sat starkers with a back brace on, and can't grab them with your dodgy arm. Bob to the rescue. All thanks to Nancy's handy tips.

She was everything to me... and the kids loved her.

Posy, being the gem that she was (and always is)

continued with Bob's training - she even downloaded a course from Groupon to help. She rented an apartment just across from the hospital and made sure that Bob and the kids were well looked after, whilst Izzy was AWOL as per usual. I could see it in her eyes that she would do anything to help me... just like I had done the same with her so many years ago. Whilst I was recovering in the hospital I spent a lot of time thinking back on Posy's cancer. I tried to focus on those good memories that we had managed to share during such a difficult childhood predicament, though sometimes the bad memories cut me to my core.

After numerous appointments, I had asked for Nancy to get hold of a few more notes from the car accident, as I had seen on '*E.R*' that sometimes revisiting the facts of an accident could help recuperate the memory.

She had obliged with my permission, and mentioned that it could take a few days for her to get hold of the documents.

Until then we carried on speaking about my past, and about Izzy a lot.

I spoke for hours about my children because quite frankly I adore them, and I also told her the story about how my sister had brought them up to be mischievous and cheeky souls – the Haribo prank with Hamilton being my prime example.

I complimented Nancy every time we met, and she blushed and tucked the strand of hair that lingered on her face behind her ear.

And one day, I kissed her on the cheek as she left and she jolted. I couldn't resist. I even shocked myself by doing it.

I knew the conditions of doctors dating their patients, but I hoped I'd be her exception. Though my confidence levels were suffering with my kinda faulty penis and bad back – I felt about eighty years old.

The next day Posy had arrived and I had told her about the kiss. She had laughed and said, "Oh c'mon you know Jodie had a thing with Mr. Michaels in high school – doctor patient things can *totally* happen. Besides, you're nearly all fixed now. Just stop waiting and chase what you want."

"I could say the same about you." I had replied, pushing her to go and find this Freddie, because I knew my sister, and I knew when she truly cared about someone.

I knew from what I'd heard and secretly googled, that Freddie was no Hamilton. He was just up Posy's street, and seemed to be the type of guy she had always deserved.

A few days later Nancy had turned up with the highly anticipated set of notes. Sitting down on the edge of my hospital bed she popped on her little rounded glasses, and began studying the notes.

But something was wrong.

"Oh no," she exhaled, "I'm sorry, Noah. This is too much. I have to go. I'm so sorry."

And so, Nancy left in a hurry leaving the folder at the base of my bed, opened, revealing every ounce of information that I had trouble remembering.

I sat in shock for a while, unable to decide whether to cry, or ignore the fact that she was the one person I had thought could be the one.

After a good half hour of numbness and not really knowing how to react to the situation, I reached to the end of my bed to try and see what this folder had inside it that had made her so upset, so scared.

Reading through the witness statements and analyzing the photos from the scene, I had a lump in my throat as flashbacks flicked through my head.

But I couldn't see anything that would have caused that reaction. Perhaps someone in her family had been in a similar situation... that was the only explanation that I could manage to summon together.

Hamilton had walked past the window on his way to see a patient for a negligence discussion, and I hesitantly hollered him over. Explaining the situation, I asked him to study the folder, looking for any reason why she had gone. Don't get me wrong, I hate Hamilton's guts but his knowledge right there and then was worth a million dollars.

"What did you say your therapists name was?" Hamilton had asked me.

"Nancy."

"But what's her full name?"

"Dr Nancy Crafton... why?"

Hamilton had exclaimed "Jackpot!" like the absolute prick he is, somewhat proud of himself for finding the matching clue.

"Dr Crafton is the sister of the bloke who hit you head on in that accident, mate."

And then Hamilton had slammed the folder shut in a businessman kind of way, before walking out of the room as if I was just another customer.

My mouth fell open in shock at the unfolded events, and quite frankly at the shit luck I had with females.

I didn't really know what to think. My heart hurt at the fact that I couldn't bring myself to fall in love with someone who was so close to someone who had nearly taken my life. I know that sounds so selfish, but my heart had already been broken once, and I couldn't figure out if I would survive another heartbreak.

Typical. The one person I felt I might be able to love was related to the guy I knew I would never love.

Chapter 21

POSY

On the Radio

I picked Niall and Jessie up in the early hours, ready for their morning flight to go and see Izzy's Mum and Dad for a few weeks' vacation. They lived in Monaco in some sort of Princess Jasmine palace.

Noah couldn't drive anymore with his condition and so I had insisted he stay at hospital with Bob, and keep working on the training I had started with him. That dog was magical. He brought a lot of happiness, mischief and company to Noah, and all of us in general. Apart from when he needed his anal glands emptying. Then I hated him with a passion. But he was so cute, so occasionally having to put my fingers up his arse to manually empty his glands wasn't all that bad.

Fred had been on my mind since the day I had walked out of the door, and I was on one of those days where you're on the verge of crying, vomiting and telling every annoying person to go fuck themselves. Yes, that's quite right – my ride was due to be under construction any day. God, periods are soooooo much fun.

Whilst driving, I switched on the radio, hoping for some kind of feel good anthem – and do you *know* what came on? "If I Let You Go" by Westlife. Even the radio was trying to upset me, and so I flicked the channel, and I heard and found something I had been longing for... *His* voice.

I saw you standing there in the darkness, you stood out in your pink converse,

We fell in love within a matter of hours, and made love in between bedsheets and showers,

I kissed you one sweet night, and when you cried I held you through the night,

You might not know this but,

I wrote a song about you baby,

Remember your red lace and my jeans on the floor,

Clumsily trying to find the switch by the door,

We couldn't wait to hold each other,

And made love in the darkness with one another,

I let you go one sweet night,

And when you left, I cried myself through the twilight,

I just wish I could see you, tonight,

You used to run your fingers along my neck, and kiss me when I didn't expect,

We had coffee and made the world ours, turning off our phones,

Now here I am watching Modern Family all alone,

I preferred it better when you were mine and I was yours,

When you sat in my apartment eating ice cream in nothing but your shorts,

You might not know this but...

I wrote a song about you baby,

Remember your red lace and my jeans on the floor,

Clumsily trying to find the switch by the door,

I don't get to hold you any more,

Missin you is my only flaw,

I try to be strong without you,

But you were the sunshine drying out my monsoon,

I just wish I could see you soon.

You fell for me baby, I fell for you,

I've got nothing left to lose,

I've already lost you,

We had the best time of our lives, didn't we, honey?

You kissed my cheek, lips like honeydew,

We can still be something, where are you?

As the song faded away. the loud Mancunian DJ explained, "And that was *The Rainer's* performing live from the studio, and yes I think we all hope a certain someone is listening to this station right here, right now."

I stopped the car in the middle of a traffic jam and didn't move. Jessie and Niall were shouting, "Aunt Posy, the lights are green so Daddy says that means we have to go!" But their voices were a faint sound as my heart pounded in my chest.

I loved him with every ounce of my body, and he felt the same. He felt the same. Oh my god. He hadn't forgotten about me. He didn't hate me for walking out on him... Oh my goooooodddddddd.

"Kids, we're taking a detour." I said and did a life changing U-Turn, abruptly turning towards the hospital.

The kids and I sat in traffic queues leading to the hospital – I was getting more and more wound up with my satnav that was stuck on the American setting that kept saying, "Do a U-Turn at the traffic circle."

IT IS A FUCKING ROUNDABOUT NOT A FUCKING TRAFFIC CIRCLE.

The kids were bickering in the back because neither of them wanted to go and see their 'boring' grandparents.

I rang Noah on speakerphone. "Noah," I said breathlessly, "I'm about to do something I should have done long ago. I'm going to come and drop the kids off with you in hospital okay? They don't want to go to see you know who anyway... I'm taking a flight to Manchester. I'm going to get Freddie back. I love him Noah and I am going to go and chase him."

"Good girl! Yes!!!!!!! Go on Posy girl. This is amazing. Sure, come bring them to me. I don't blame them for not wanting to go and see The Royals in Monaco anyway. I, err, I have a visitor right now, the nurse has just informed me, but just bring them along. This is so mad Posy. But I *know* you love him. Don't think twice. *Do it* Mrs." Noah replied, a spring in his step evident in his voice.

~

We finally reached the hospital and the kids, latching onto each of my hands, ran with me to their Dad's room.

"Hi!" I squealed, frankly out of breath from legging it up about eight flights of stairs, and dragging two children along with me. I had the urge to vomit and released myself in the bin, the excitement and exhilaration evident, and also my lack of stamina...

Noah was not alone – there was a fair-haired, familiar man sat beside him. He stood up to greet me.

"So, I guess I'll just put it out there and introduce myself... I'm Noah's real Dad."

He continued, "I had no idea that Noah even existed until the other day...I understand you have something you need to go and do. Leave the kids here, it would be nice to get to know my grandchildren. Go Posy. Go."

He spoke so softly, so coarsely. It was as if I knew him already, somehow...

I smiled, and saw the pride in his eyes. I didn't even catch his name before I left, but I liked him nonetheless.

I quickly kissed Noah on the forehead and waved goodbye to my niece and nephew who were screaming, "Run Aunty Posy! Run!"

And boy did I run. I ran down the flights of stairs wheezing, with my lack of fitness suddenly becoming evident. My boobs were jiggling and nearly knocking me out as I got nearer to the bottom of the staircase – they'd gotten bigger recently. Not that I was going to complain.

~

After a two-hour bumper-to-bumper taxi drive, I reached the airport just in time for the midafternoon flight to Manchester, and then it hit me.

I didn't have any money on me. Or my phone. It was all in my car at the hospital.

Shit, shit, shit.

Thinking quick I ran over to a businessman in what looked like the Armani suit Hamilton used to wear, and babbled on about how I really needed to borrow £50 for a flight to go and see the love of my life before he got back on a plane to Arizona, but he wouldn't budge. Fucking posh wanker.

And so, I miserably tried for a good hour to try and grab some cash off of every rich person I saw, or anyone that looked generous. But no-one would even consider me. Mind you, I did look like a begging hippie with my hair all unattractively stuck to my forehead, after my hike up the hospital stairs.

After a good effort and no one even bothering to help me in my begging quest, I swallowed my pride and gave up. Sitting down on one of the metal chairs in the arrivals area, I had a little cry. I had missed him. He would be on the plane back home to Arizona by now, back in a land far away from little old me.

Why had I let him go? I sunk back into the leatherette chair and stared blankly into the distance, not really sure whether to move or stay there forever.

But then... I heard my name being shouted from behind the immigrations check in. I knew the voice.

Oh. My. Fucking. Jesus. God. Lord.

BANG.

Chapter 22

FREDDIE

Barriers

I could see her. She was literally a few steps away, but I couldn't - no matter how hard I pushed and pushed - get to her.

As soon as I had finished singing one of the many songs that I had written about her at *MAN FM* I had literally raced to the nearest airport. I had thought with my heart for once, and didn't let my head or my negative thoughts stop me.

As I was singing the words, I realized all along that she was the one for me. Ever since that Robbie Williams song had informed me in *Gatsby's* – she's the *one.*

I think perhaps I was so afraid of heartbreak, of losing someone again, and I ran. I ran as far away from a problem because I couldn't bear to be a part of it, for fear of going back to that dark place. I let my insecurities get the better of me, as I often do, and I nearly let her go. The power of music and lyrics can help you to realize a lot in life, so don't ever forget to stop and listen.

When I landed at Gatwick, all around me were fans screaming my name, and security had gone mental saying no one could pass through the Arrivals security checks for fear of my safety. *The Rainer's* were up and coming at that point, and the screaming teenage (occasionally psychotic) girls were a side effect of it.

But then through the swarm of screaming fans I saw her.

I was shouting her name, and all of a sudden, she heard me. I forgot about all the assumptions I had made about her and Hamilton, and kicked myself for not thinking more highly of her.

Her puppy-dog brown eyes gazed longingly for me as we clocked one another through the glass barrier between us. It was like a scene written for a movie with an unhappy ending, but I would make sure that it didn't end there, and that I didn't lose sight of her again.

In a midst of screaming girls, she was the one dressed quirkier than ever in a flowery dungaree number, and all I wanted to do was run and run until I reached her. But I couldn't. There was no chance in hell one guy could push through a crowd of screaming, touchy girls.

Thinking quickly, I pulled my phone out of my pocket and texted her – just as the security dragged me into a side room – saying I would meet her back at the hospital where I knew her brother was... and that I was sorry.

Just as I was being hauled into the side room by Tony - the big scary security guard we'd recently employed - a screaming fan threw her bra at me. Way to be brought back to the reality of fame, right? Posy had been different to all of those girls that threw items of clothing at me on stage, and for that I loved and respected her even more than was humanly possible.

Suddenly I heard a bang, the ground was shaking, shrapnel flying toward me and then everything went black.

My last thought was, *Posy.*

~

I could hear people shouting, "There's been a terrorist attack!"

My eyes were slowly coming back into clarity, and then my instincts kicked in as I tried to stand, my leg searing with pain.

I had various PO's rushing over to me trying to tell me that I couldn't leave the room for fear of my safety and life. They thought I was a possible target.

Bollocks to that I'd thought. It's not about me, it's about Posy, it's about all of those people lying out there, injured, and for the first time in my life I *prayed*, and I prayed those affected were casualties, and not fatalities.

I snuck under my bodyguard Tony's huge, bulging arm and ran as fast as I could to the fire exit. I felt like a convict escaping Alcatraz. My leg dragged slightly along the crumbling floor beneath me. My sight was impaired by the layers and layers of smoke.

I was scared shitless.

Just ahead of me, I saw a young boy, who must have been around two years old, screaming. He wasn't injured but I could see he needed some sort of human touch to remind him that everything would be ok. So, I scooped him up into my arms, cradling his head as he rested it, almost in exhaustion, on my shoulder.

Then I ran towards the smoke.

In the smoky distance, I saw Posy leaning over a poor young girl whose leg was in a bad shape and I rushed over to her, with both relief and shock, kissing her, "God you're okay, you're okay baby."

And then, gripping one another's hand we helped as many people as we could, comforted many who were in tears, including young children screaming for their Mummies and Daddies.

Looking around I could just see a floor covered in people screaming out, and I also saw kind humans running towards them, risking their own life for a stranger.

Sometimes, seeing that kindness of humanity secures your trust in the world being a nice place, despite the cruelty within it also.

I don't know how to describe how I was feeling in that moment - I try not to hate anything because it's such a strong and resentful emotion. But anyone who has the intention to kill innocent lives, frankly the emotion of hatred doesn't even cover it.

~

A few weeks later it was revealed that it was a British Man of just twenty-nine, who had set off a pipe bomb in the airport.

He was Anti-Muslim and it was classed as a hate crime.

He was intending to kill every Muslim in the airport that day, because he believed they were all brainwashed and terrorists. In truth, the only terrorist was himself.

Islam is such a beautiful religion - Mum had told me all about it when describing her travels to Bangladesh and Indonesia. It's the misinterpretation of religion that often causes the most hurt.

The numbers were two hundred casualties and miraculously zero fatalities, it was revealed on the news as Posy and I sat in the back of an ambulance, along with the young girl Posy had rescued from the wreckage. Posy held the young girl's hand, mothering her whilst a paramedic strapped my leg up, which was covered in lesions from the shrapnel. Posy seemed to know the paramedic in the ambulance - she told me, "His name is Cody. It's a long, but funny story I'll tell you all about him one day."

During the ride to the hospital my mind was blurred, every miscommunication melted away as I held Posy and knew that what I'd assumed could never be true.

The bomb had made me realize just how close anyone can be to the end, at any point. Holding your feelings back is not something we have time for.

If you love someone, tell them.

We didn't say anything, we just held each other and she cried into the curve of my shoulder.

Both of us were in a daze at how far we'd come and how long it had been since we'd been together.

Whatever you do in love, never assume. Because assuming causes miscommunications that cause an unbearable amount of heartbreak. Trust me, I know, first-hand.

When we arrived at the hospital, the young girl was wheeled into surgery, her small hand squeezed mine as she was whisked away. I gripped Posy's hand as we walked through the busy scene of the hospital. I don't quite think anyone could believe how anyone had survived the blast. I was bombarded with reporters and various DCI's who thought that I was the target. The truth was, the target was me and every other innocent person in that airport. It's sickening to think about it. Even to this day I can't recall how anyone can think mass killing is going to result in greater happiness for the greater good.

Focusing on Posy's hand in mine I took a moment to think. Hand holding is a rather magical thing, so simplistic, but also something that makes your heart skip so many beats. A simple movement of the hand can say a lot about a person, and in some cases, it may well be the indicator that that's the hand you want to always be there to hold.

Strangers may kiss, or sleep together, but many don't hold hands.

That's something precious that you save for someone who has the potential to become more than a stranger.

I paused as we were walking in through the hospital doors, as the police cordoned off the press and reporters; I felt I needed to apologize. "I'm so sorry," was all I could fumble together.

"Sorry for what honey? It's all my fault – I left you with no explanation, and I was so unexplainably horrible to you. Don't you dare apologize to me, you've done nothing. I just feel lucky that you've given me a second chance."

"No honey, don't apologize for that. Your brother nearly died, Jesus we nearly just died. You had every right to tell me what you did, and I don't hate you for it. In fact, I thank you because you made me realize that love was worth chasing again..."

I took a deep breath before carrying on with my monologue, "I got on the next plane after you left from Barcelona, and I came right here, but then I saw you kissing Hamilton, and then I rang you and he picked up and I just assumed... I'm so sorry."

"Oh honey. No, there is no chance in hell that man is ever coming near to me again. I am so sorry you saw that Hamilton came onto me and I was feeling so lonely and vulnerable and let him kiss me, and I fell for him because I wanted to forget about the fact that I had hurt you so bad, that I didn't deserve you anymore. And then I realized that his kiss was nothing compared to yours, and I also found him in bed with my sister in law... I know, long story babe... And most importantly, I can't believe that dickhead didn't tell me you'd rang. I am so sorry that I broke your heart so many times. But thank you for coming back to me. Life wasn't life without you."

Suddenly every single miscommunication was explained within a matter of minutes, and everything fell into place.

"My Dad once told me that if you ever let a girl walk away from you, then it's a mistake you'll forever regret. So, you have my Dad to thank when you meet him." I whispered, kissing her soft lips.

Pulling me in through the hospital doors, Posy babbled on about how excited Noah was to see me, her hair was covered in dust and her eyebrow was bleeding still.

We had informed the detective on the scene of our statements, and said we would return later for more questioning. Posy had also rung Noah immediately as she didn't want him to have a heart attack - she told him we were both safe. Thank God.

From what Posy was telling me on our way to Noah's room, she had been telling Noah all about me and I felt so appreciated. I know that's such a weird feeling to try and explain, but it doesn't happen often...

Right there, in that moment, I had everything I could ever need, and ever want... and I realized a lot had changed, in such little time, and I would never change it for the whole world.

She pulled me into the little side room where Noah was sitting up in bed, a huge smile of relief spreading across his face, seeing his sister, alive ... and then...

Looking across at the man sat on the little chair beside Noah, I was suddenly confused.

"Dad, what are you doing here?"

Chapter 23

NOAH

Two of a kind

"**W**hat's going on?" I asked my recently acclaimed Dad, baffled that this guy Posy absolutely adored had just called *my* Dad, *Dad*. Was I going crazy? I swore my memory wasn't that bad.

Jessie and Niall seemed completely unaware of the situation unfolding around them. They were both running around my hospital wash room with Bob following them in circles. I couldn't stop thinking how they could have been at the airport, if it hadn't been for Posy making that life-changing and life-saving U-Turn.

My new Dad looked just as confused as everyone else in the room. Fred looked at me, then back at my new Dad, then Posy looked at Fred, Posy then looked at me... but then we were all drawn to the voice at the door.

My Mum suddenly stood still as a statue just before the threshold and whispered, "Oh my goodness, Harvey...Harvey Bayer... is that really you?"

Shit the bed was my first thought. And also, where was *MTV Pranked* when you needed them... Surely it was all a joke... some big misunderstanding. Fred couldn't have the same Dad as me... talk about a freaky coincidence.

Posy taking a deep breath, and screwing up the skin between her eyebrows with her fingertips, suddenly said, "Wait a minute, Mum... does this mean that Noah's real Dad, Harvey, is Fred's adoptive father?"

Mum slowly nodded and everyone in the room just stared at one another in turn. Somewhat surprised at the closeness of us all, all of a sudden.

Then Posy, thinking harder said "So that makes Freddie, Noah's brother... well, kind of?"

And Mum and Harvey looked at one another, exchanging silent words, and nodded slowly, assessing the situation.

Then Mum had suddenly said an expletive which

was rare for her and looking at Freddie and Posy exclaimed, "Oh god, so you two being together is quite frankly incest."

Posy laughed out loud and turned to Mum before turning to face Freddie, disrupting the disordered silence that had encased the room and said, "No Mum. I just thank fuck they're not related by blood, and am so glad you were adopted," she laughed cuddling into Freddie, "Because otherwise that could have been a little bit of a problem."

Harvey looked completely bewildered by the fact that his new son's sister, was dating his adoptive son. Freddie was from Arizona, and Posy from Kent, and they'd crossed one another's paths in Barcelona. It was complete and utter madness, in its most beautiful form.

Suddenly everyone in the room's blank expressions turned into a smile and I sat totally mesmerized by the fact that not only had I just gained myself another father... but also a brother.

Freddie, never properly having met me before, made his way over to me and shook my hand, before saying, "Good to meet you Bro. From what Posy's said so far, you sound like the type of guy I will be proud to be related to."

He had blood staining his fingertips and a nasty gash across his forehead. I was ultimately blown away by how everybody from the bombing was okay. I couldn't stop thinking about how different things could have been.

I had returned Freddie's firm, brotherly, respectful handshake and winked at him, "You look after her, ok. Or I'll break your face. Just kidding, my leftie doesn't even work anymore. But I will still break you. Be warned."

He had smiled kindly at me and nodded his understanding, and for some reason I immediately became protective over him. He was, by definition my little brother, and I had a responsibility to look after him... and I knew in my heart that he'd be the person that made Posy the happiest little lady on earth.

Harvey stood up to properly introduce himself to Posy, his opening line being, "So I see you've met my sons?" and she had giggled before saying, "Yes I certainly have, and I love them both dearly."

Letting go of Freddie, Posy ran over to me to kiss my forehead and hold me tight.

"I love you little one." I whispered, just as a tsunami of invading kids came and jumped on their favourite Aunty.

Chapter 24

NOAH

Damn you, Freddie

I kept the whole episode with Nancy to myself for a while - I just didn't want people feeling even more sorry for me. Pity is something I never want, because the reality is that I'm never going to be able to move my arm again, and my brain isn't working as well as it should be.

But sometimes that's how life goes, and we just have to deal with that... right?

But the secret about what had happened with Nancy was uncovered one evening by Freddie, who had come over to see me in hospital. He had been visiting daily after he and Posy had found one another again.

Though at first I was happy for them, over the passing days following their reunion, I couldn't help but feel resentment towards the fact that I wanted Nancy and I to have what they had too. I wanted to try again with her, but I just couldn't accept the fact that her brother had nearly killed me.

I know it was silly for me to try and say that I really loved Nancy because I had only known her for a few weeks... but hey, look at my sister! Ha-ha! She is totally gonna kill me for saying that...

Freddie had managed to wangle the truth out of me one evening when he was asking about how I was *really* doing. Emphasis on the really there. He was someone who I could talk to about anything, without feeling as if he would judge me... and I truly respected him for it.

He'd told me that life doesn't just end after one love ends, and that if everybody assumed that it did, the world would be empty. He had this ability of coaxing a lot of information out of me that I usually wouldn't have told a soul. It felt different suddenly having this brother who I felt comfortable talking too; the bond was almost immediate.

He'd also been asking about Izzy a lot - I assumed that Posy had been telling him that I wasn't myself and that I needed a good grown up talk with another man - and on that day, I felt ready to open up.

I told him about my suspicions over the years, and how it made it even worse knowing that she'd put the kids second too. I told him about the evenings where I would sit waiting up for her to come back from a so-called shift, knowing that she was actually busy in other respects.

He listened intently and answered with a reply that made it clear to me why Posy had fallen for him, "Sometimes, Noah, we get so wrapped up in our own worlds that we forget that someone, out there, is feeling just the same. But you know what is the most important thing to remember? If you find someone you do truly love, then you won't ever hurt them, and you'll do everything you possibly can to keep them in your life. Because, in truth, you wouldn't ever hurt someone that you truly love."

We had sat up speaking way past the visiting hours, and I had opened up about Nancy. I hadn't told a soul about the discovery.

Posy had known that something was up because I went from talking about Nancy, Nancy, Nancy to avoiding hearing or speaking her name.

I told Freddie how I couldn't find it in my heart to love someone who had been so close to someone who had very nearly virtually killed me. And that I felt incredibly horrible and selfish for seeing her as a bad person, just because she was related to one.

He totally understood where I was coming from and said that he could understand why I felt the way I did. Accepting someone into your life is never easy.

But then Freddie opened my eyes to something.

He reminisced, "When I was younger, I got hurt by so many girls because I couldn't spell, and because I didn't have perfect teeth, and I actually started to resent girls as a whole for being so shallow. But then I realized that that was just a generalisation - I was assuming that all girls would never love me because I had flaws... So, I guess what I'm trying to say is that Nancy and her brother are two different people, so don't generalise too much. And don't let yourself be misogynistic just because of Izzy. If you love Nancy, don't make the mistake of letting someone else have her... because she's not him, and he's not her."

In that moment, I realized that I had made the mistake of letting someone go because I'd assumed she wasn't who I thought she was.
But the truth was, you can be related to someone, yet entirely different. I mean, look at me and Posy and Freddie... we are dissimilar in our own ways. We are all good for something, in our own ways.

And so, with Fred's wise words and a kick up the arse, I hopped into my wheelchair and Fred pushed me towards reception.

"Excuse me Nurse, please can I make an appointment with Nancy, this afternoon?"

"Erm, she's requested that she not see you."

"I know," I said, thinking carefully about how to word exactly what I wanted to say, "Just tell her it's ok, and to meet me at our usual time, usual place."

~

I waited and I waited, but Nancy never showed. I was crushed, completely and utterly defeated by every hope Fred had given me that she'd come running back.

I rang him up and told him that she hadn't showed up, and he said, "I'm sorry Noah. Maybe she just needs a little more time. If it's the real thing, then it'll happen, alright?"

Fred insisted on coming over to sit with me in the hospital, but I felt like a bit of a burden and so told him not to. He showed up ironically, bringing along with him contraband of beer and potato chips – the cure for heartbreak sometimes I suppose. He seemed to have the same feistiness of my sister, and I really appreciated that.

Posy, Niall and Jessie showed up a half an hour later with more contraband, which included Bob the puppy. I thought in that moment how I'd got everything I'd ever really need right there and then, and my thoughts drifted away from Nancy for a while as I talked and laughed to the people who had always stuck by me.

I watched Fred and Posy with each other and they had *it;* that thing that everyone hopes they'll one day have, and it took my breath away. I felt a lump in my throat as I saw my duty to protect her was no longer needed because she'd found someone who would love her endlessly, forever. A proud and emotional big brother moment for sure.

As Niall and Jessie went to take Bobby out for his toilet break (which Posy informed me wasn't going to well at her place, after Bobby had left some explosive diarrhea up the wall whilst she was out), Posy and Fred both sat on either side of my bed.

"Are you alright Noah?" Posy asked, gently stroking my head.

A tear ran down my face, "I don't really know anymore Posy. I just hope she might change her mind... but I have you guys, and that's a lot to be thankful for."

She kissed me on the cheek, and Freddie gave me one of his special, "*It's going to be okay mate*" hugs. Posy and Freddie walked out of the hospital room hand in hand. I just hoped Nancy would give me another chance and that she thought with her heart, because I believed that we had what they had. Love.

Chapter 25

POSY

If you do, I do too

As with any shotgun love, comes a shotgun wedding.

One autumn morning, Fred had woken up, turned over and whispered, "Marry me?" I kissed him in response thinking he was joking and said, "Oh go on then, you're not so bad I guess."

Then he had gotten out of bed, and reached into his suitcase.

"What are you doing their baby?" I inquired curiously.

"Well, truth be told I decided I was going to propose to you about a week after we met... I know, you can call me crazy but I just knew when I saw you that it was going to be us for the rest of our days."

He turned around, crouching down beside the bed, the early morning sun blazing across his collarbone. In his hand was a ring I had always dreamed of.

"It was my Mum's engagement ring."

I broke down and cried, tears streaming down my face, "I love it Freddie. It's beautiful. Are you sure she would want me to have it?"

I could not take my eyes off the tear-drop shaped Ruby ring he had placed on my ring finger.

He kissed me slow and his lips lingered for a moment before he said, "She would have loved you Posy. And she would have loved for you to have it, because truth be told you make her son so happy it's unreal."

He climbed back into bed, his legs straddling me and kissed me again and again, his hands stroking the base of my neck.

Then he stopped, his eyes bright with one of this many crazy ideas - remember that time we got matching tattoos? My Nana wasn't too impressed...

"How about we get married tonight?" He spontaneously offered, looking directly and intensely into my eyes.

Then he began serenading a very tired me with, "We've got tonight. Who needs tomorrow?" in his beautifully crafted voice.

And quoting from Bob Seger himself, he won my heart, my soul and utter admiration for him, and so it was settled: a morning proposal, midday prep and an evening wedding.

We jumped up out of bed, both naked from last night's magical love-making session, and suddenly ruining the moment entirely, I had to run to the toilet to throw up.

Fred ran after me, on hair-holding patrol, whilst wiping my mouth with a tissue. He rubbed the base of my back as he always does to calm me, and poured me some water from the sink, efficiently emptying the toothbrush holder to use as a glass.

"Baby what did you eat?" He asked, concerned.

"Well, I don't think it's what I ate," I stated nervously, and took a big breath before continuing.

I'd received some results the day previous.

"I went for a checkup yesterday morning, it's a yearly thing with my leukemia. You know when I told you I was home marking work…Well I told you a bit of a white lie because I didn't want to worry you. In short, they found something Fred. An inconclusive result. In my stomach."

"Baby, no, no. You should've told me," Fred hugged me close.

I felt unbelievably cruel playing my little game with him before revealing the big truth, but talk about making something memorable, right?

"And they said I have nine months. Until they'll know if they can remove it."

"Baby, what are you saying?" Fred said, suddenly doing the math on my nine-month hint, before the realization hit, and he did a double take at my little plump belly.

"Oh my god, baby! Whaaaaaattttt, we're having a baby! But you said that... You couldn't... Wow... How did this happen... I mean, I *know* how it happens... But you can't... Baby, you know what, it's meant to be... It's the greatest news I've ever heard... And quite frankly I must have some fucking super sperm, right?"

"Oh, don't flatter yourself... Daddy." I whispered, gently kissing him on the cheek. We both sat slumped on the damp bathroom floor, our bare feet intertwined.

"You know I *thought* your boobs had gotten bigger. But I wasn't going to complain. I like your body no matter what shape or form it comes in, it's those eyes that I won't ever allow to change. They're the reason I first fell for you. Oh, and those pink shoes.

Which you might not be able to fit in to soon because of those swollen ankles..." He joked, laughing at his own little witticism.

I opened my mouth in shock, and laughed as Fred continued to say, "But for right now, we have some time to celebrate our morning engagement, morning sickness and evening wedding, right? Oh, and don't hesitate to call me Daddy as much as you want..." He whispered, cheekily using his hands to touch my sensitive body that shivered at his touch, and he kissed my neck, making me moan...

I pushed his hand away from my knicker line and said, "No no no, Freddie, when the party ends we can, but right now, *this* is regrettably off limits."

Leaving him gasping and wanting me, I grabbed my bag, and threw an outfit on before kissing his smiling face.

"I love you, Freddie Bayer. I look forward to our next meeting."

~

Noah, Jessie and Niall received our news via Skype, but only the wedding news; we left the baby news out because I wasn't that far along, and I felt as if I was treading on eggshells already with my apparent, yet highly false infertility status.

After receiving our call, Nat and Jodie flew in from New York, Andy the Spanish waiter from *Gatsby's* flew in from Spain and Harvey caught a flight in from Arizona as soon as he heard the news.

Dymphna, my Waterford friend, and her lovely family flew in without a moment's hesitation and it all just fell into place. Even Augustina my old Spanish neighbor hopped on a flight to come and be a part of our big day. She was so relieved that I was no longer a spinster.

The fellow *Rainer's* were flying in too (my arrangement, that Fred had *no* idea about), and even Mum and Dad said that they would be making the hour drive to see us get married, picking my Nana up on the way... the one who used to be convinced I was asexual. She was pretty set in her ways; the moment she found out that I was best friends with a lesbian, she nearly fainted in shock. Yes, Nan, a *lesbian. God* help me.

Freddie organized most of the wedding and he chose that at 8.30pm we would get married under the stars, nothing fancy, or so he told me that.

Ironically, 8:30pm was the time of our first date, except it was postponed after I fell over outside of *Gatsby's* and shouted, "Oh Fuck!" at the top of my lungs.

Our whole relationship from start to finish was totally unplanned, spontaneous, yet destined, and the wedding preparations (or lack of) represented us two to a tee.

~

Jodie and Nat arrived early afternoon, and Nat headed straight for our secret venue to set up lighting and music like the absolute angel she is, leaving me and Jodie alone to shop for the big evening.

Freddie mentioned that he knew the perfect place where he wanted to marry me, and I so left it to him.

He joked with me that all he had to do was put on a red blazer and tight trousers and he knew I'd marry him, *and* that us girls needed a little longer than he did to get ready for the wedding. Arguably true. Not many men offer to take on that big a responsibility, but my only requirement was tight trousers so he couldn't have been imperfect if he'd tried.

I trusted him with my heart, body and soul, and to be honest I wouldn't have minded getting married in a muddy farm – as *long* as there weren't any pigs that is... Flashbacks to Theo's house-sitting experience still haunt me to this day...

Jodie and I took a train into Soho late morning, heading straight for our favourite charity shops,

knowing quite well that every wedding boutique in London had a 20-week consultation waiting list.

Ain't nobody got time for that.

Besides, charity shops have some absolute steals hidden, and they're just waiting to be found by people who have a flare for distinctiveness. AKA Jodie and I.

We searched through racks and racks and I tried on the ugliest pastry shaped frocks, until we found the perfect dress. Jodie had picked it out whilst I had ummed and ahhed over whether I could actually pull it off, but then it fit like an absolute dream.

It also reminded me of *The Great Gatsby* movie with Carey Mulligan and Leonardo DiCaprio, taking me back to our first date at *Gatsby*'s. It was a blush pink number. Oh, and just a side note seeing as I have the opportunity here - if my life story ever gets made into a movie, Leonardo DiCaprio, you're hired...

We then began looking through piles and piles of shoes, but they were all too big, or too high or too white, and then swiftly an idea hit me. If Fred was wearing his red blazer, then it would only be right to wear my pink Converse, especially before my ankles turned into balloons...

Jodie had been in the changing room helping me to

zip up my dress when she noticed that I was a little rounder than usual. "God who ate all the pies Posy? Wait... You're not, *you know*, are you?"

I took a deep breath and thought about my fear of

not telling anyone until I knew for sure it wasn't all a dream, but Jodie looked at me sincerely, genuinely wanting to know if all of my dreams had come true at once.

I smiled and nodded shyly, "Magically, yes... but shhh, don't tell anyone."

Jodie's jaw dropped to the ground.

"I'm going to be an Aunty. Oh my god, my best friend is knocked up!"

"Not just an Aunt, Jodie. Godmother, too. *Fairy* Godmother."

Her eyes moistened with the beginnings of tears as she bent down to hug my belly, kneeling down before me she whispered to the little person inside me, "Let's get Cinderella to the ball, hey little one."

~

Fred had text Jodie to inform her that she needed to get me onto the Isle of Sheppy by 8pm, and Fred being aware of my fear of boats told me that he'd be waiting on the other side, unlike Jack Dawson who'd gone down with the ship... I seem to be on a roll with my Leonardo DiCaprio references here...

My fear of boats is legit though. I had a panic attack watching *Moana* with Jessie and Niall.

They found it hilarious.

Freddie always listened to me when I told him about my life and my memories; he knew that the Isle of Sheppy was The Island that Dad, Noah and I used to visit. It was my happy place.

And I couldn't wait to make more memories that I couldn't ever possibly forget.

After trying to get out of London in rush hour train traffic, we finally made it back to my apartment with just enough time to have a quick shower. Jodie was an absolute star and did my makeup and hair whilst we chatted about her wanting to propose to Natalie in the near future. We had both found happiness at last, and boy did we deserve every bit of it.

There was a knock at the door and a delivery man showed up with two glittery, yellow umbrellas. We were instructed to take them with us. The sky didn't look grey, and the forecast looked ok, but maybe Fred was just taking precaution... or maybe he had something else up his sleeve.

Just as we were calling for a taxi after getting dressed and make-upped within an hour (good going, I know), there was another knock at the door.

It was my Dad. His mouth dropped open as he took

in my outfit, tearing up.

"Oh Kiddo, you look so beautiful," he whispered, pulling me into an embrace and stroking my hair gently like he used too before I grew up and got boobs and emotions, and all that shit.

"I'm here to take you to an Island far, far away." He said magically, moving away from the door threshold to reveal a Corvette in the driveway.

"And this my dear, is your carriage."

My heart melted like an ice cream cone on a hot summer's day. Fred had remembered my Corvette story, and Dad was helping make it come true. I turned back to look at Jodie who had both hands on her cheeks, staring in awe at her best friend, all grown up before her.

"C'mon Mrs," I uttered, "Can't start the wedding without my Maid of Honour beside me."

Chapter 26

POSY

I must be dreaming

The Corvette drove like an absolute dream, the hum of the engine combined with my butterflies made quite the melody. Jodie had her head out of the window in the front seat like an excitable puppy, the dull skies becoming brighter because of her happiness. My Dad sat driving proudly.

Dad couldn't tell me where exactly we were going when we reached the Isle of Sheppy, and it reminded me of that *Don't Tell the Bride* programme I used to binge watch when Hamilton was 'out'. 'Out' meaning bonking some young brunette with a Vajazzle. I even got my Mum addicted to it – the programme that is, not vajazzles. Oh god, now I can't unsee what I've just seen. Mums and Vajazzles. No. No. And no.

The sky looked a little unsettled and I laughed to myself as I suddenly clicked with the umbrella theme – rain.

Rain had been the making of us, we had both had raindrop tattoos and we had both spent endless nights curled up in one another's arms, listening to the sound of the pitter patter of rain, on the window. Oh, and not to forget the joyful moment where the rain had caused me to slip and go flying on our first official date. Thank you, Rain.

Rain also metaphorically washes away the bad stuff and makes things grow again. I guess Fred was rain for me. He helped me to grow and I was indeed in full bloom. Literally.

Jodie squealed with excitement as we reached the crossing and all piled into the little boat. Climbing on board, I remember feeling very thankful for my shoe choice – ain't nobody going to be wearing stilettos on a boat with holes in, unless you want to die, that is.

After a choppy crossing and me praying to a God – I hadn't prayed since childhood Sunday School - for my life, and having had a brief panic attack, we managed to get to the type of surface that you can stand on without sinking.

It had started spitting a little as we made our way up to where there was a sign in the shape of a raindrop, with the word 'Clue' written on it.

God, I may not have been marrying Gerard Butler, but that was seriously some *P.S. I Love You* kind of shit.

The clue said:

> *You know I'm no good at spelling,*
>
> *But I know how to spell love,*
>
> *Because you are like a dictionary,*
>
> *You just need to look up 'above'*

With my heart melting in my chest, I tilted my umbrella to see the sight above me. And truth be told – I very nearly started blubbering right there and then.

There was a handmade glittery sign that looked very Noah and Jessie-esque that said, "Welcome to *Gatsby's*" and there, stood with another clue, was no other than Andy the wise Barcelonan waiter.

Absolutely gob smacked by that point, Dad and Jodie holding onto each arm, took me up a little set of steps to go and collect the next clue that Andy seemed to be holding.

It said:

> *I fell for a girl called Posy when in Spain,*
>
> *But we're in Kent, so put up your umbrella,*

In case there's any rain

And just as I had finished reading the last line, smiling uncontrollably, from above floated down yellow, sparkly flakes of confetti cascading in beautiful spirals.

A huge balloon also floated down and on it was written another clue. Jodie was as mesmerized as me, and Dad was wearing one hell of a smile on his face.

The clue said:

This balloon is yellow,

My jacket is red,

You requested tight jeans,

So just take one last step

And taking one last step, I looked up to see Freddie stood at the edge of the mezzanine, wearing no other than what he had worn when we had first met.

I saw him smile at my outfit choice, and we exchanged a glance that said a million words.

He had done it all for me. He had done the most simplistic of things and made a masterpiece out of it. Love can be anyone's masterpiece if they make the simplicities worthwhile.

Life was but a dream in that moment and I couldn't quite believe how quickly my life had gone from being a miserable singleton, to becoming someone's to love, someone else's reason to live again.

Dad crushed my arm so hard as he realized his little girl was about to get married again, to a man (and not a complete and utter wanker) that would be hers and she his, forever.

Jodie kissed me on the cheek and headed up to Fred – with a spring in her step - who guided her to stand next to Natalie, Jessie and Niall. Natalie looked gorgeous in a slim-fitted gold sequined dress, Jessie wore a little flower halo in her hair and had a little flowy blue dress on, and Niall had a bow tie on that made him look unbelievably cuter than usual. And there in Niall's arms was Bob in a blue bow tie, wriggling around, desperate to chase the falling confetti. It warmed my heart to see what Freddie had created in less than a day. I couldn't believe my eyes.

As Dad and I made our way further up to the mezzanine, I saw my brother stood beside Fred. My heart very nearly melted; Fred had asked him to be the best man.

And beside Noah was Josh, Freddie's best friend from school and his right-hand man in *The Rainer's*, playing a melody on his guitar as I walked down the aisle. He played *"Alone"* by Eagle Eye Cherry, and it fitted our little story just perfectly.

And on the back row I noticed a familiar face... I presumed Fred had something to do with her being there.

Taking my first step down the glittery carpet piece, my ankles started shaking and a few tears fell down my cheeks. I could see Fred crying in front of me too. They were tears that showed us both how long we had waited to find one another.

From the corner of my eye I could see so many friends and family, some new and some old, stood mesmerized at the connection Freddie and I had. We intensely stared at one another as I got closer and closer to him, I suddenly couldn't wait any longer, and I ran so fast to the edge of the mezzanine and jumped into his arms.

All of the guests laughed and applauded, throwing confetti at us as we held each other so tightly. My Dad came up behind me and passed my shaky hand into Freddie's equally nervous one and said, "You take care of my little lady, Freddie, I can see a lot of love in those eyes of yours, and I give you my personal permission to stay with her for the rest of your life."

Dad kissed me gently on the cheek and shook Fred's hand before he went and took a seat next to Mum. My brother smiled at me and gave me a cheeky wink before mouthing, "He's awesome."

He and Fred had gotten to know one another so ·

well, and it was crazy how alike they were. By definition they were brothers, and in my eyes, they were both people I couldn't picture a life without. Both held a special place in my heart and will do forever.

I looked back to see my Dad smiling ear to ear, and stood in awe of what was in front, beside and behind me.

Jodie stuck her tongue out when I looked at her, and Jessie and Niall followed suit. Such a bad influence. God, I love her.

I stood considering how much had changed since the last time I'd stood at the top of the aisle. And I also considered how lucky I was to be standing there. A few weeks before my life could have been cruelly taken away from me. I could have lost Freddie, my world.

Our wedding was so unbelievably simplistic the second time around, completely unplanned, completely spontaneous and everything I could ever want.

And there was another difference too.

The guy stood in front of me had never cheated on me, or hurt me. And I loved him. He also happened to be the father of the little baby growing inside of me.

A lot had changed. And boy was I glad it had.

Chapter 27

FREDDIE

Lucky doesn't even cover it

She looked like a beautiful pink rose as she stood before me, her soft cheeks blushed as I smiled shyly at her, and our hands nervously fidgeted with one another with eager anticipation for what the rest of our lives held.

We knew for one that a baby was first on the agenda following the news of the morning... and looking at Posy's cascading belly, I remember thinking that it wouldn't be staying a secret for long.

I could see her little bump peeking through the flowy pink dress she had on, and I beamed with pride.

Inside her was something we had made together, half me and half of the woman I loved. Love can make a lot of things, and making something with the person you love is as magical as your first time visiting Disneyland… perhaps even more magical.

It had been a long day, but I wouldn't have been able to do most of it without Noah. We had clicked immediately and his ideas bounced off mine, and Posy did agree with us that we had been able to create something memorable and worthwhile, within just a few hours.

Noah had been my obvious choice for best man because quite frankly I had adored and respected him since the first time Posy had told me about him. He cared for her like a brother should, and was extra protective with who she was allowed to love. Plus, he said I was what she had always been looking for amongst the frogs.

Finding a vicar for the shotgun wedding had been difficult at last minute's notice, but luckily life worked in my favour that day.

Andy the Spanish Waiter had trained to be a Minister in Barcelona when he was younger, and then decided he wanted to make a living in the restaurant business.

He had been only too pleased to accept my favour. 'Andy the Ledge' is what he likes to be called these days.

~

Taking a shaky deep breath, I started reading my vows to Posy, and her eyes stared at me lovingly, speaking the depths of a constellation.

"Posy. I remember the first time you kissed me; do you know why? Because your lips tasted like home. They tasted like a place I had been searching and longing for. You know I'm no good with reading or spelling, so excuse me if I stumble. Our paths crossed at a time in our lives when we had lost trust in love ever finding us again. But then, it did. My dear, I vow to forever wear tight jeans whenever you request it," I began, as the guests began chuckling away, including Posy.

"I vow to never break your heart and write endless songs about your eyes. I vow to be the one person you can rely on throughout anything, and I personally promise to pick you up when you fall and accidentally say the F word. I'll be yours forever. Pinkie promise."

She took a big sigh and whispered in my ear, "How in the world do I top that?" before beginning her vows.

With her shaky hands grasping onto the little piece of paper in her hands, she read, "Freddie. I vow to always provide in car entertainment on our road trips, even if you do insist I'm tone deaf... I promise to be there to listen and to laugh when you need me. I promise to be the light switch in a dark room when you need a guiding hand," she said, winking at me.

"I will forever remember the first time we met because you turned my entire world into a world where I wanted to fall in love again. If it wasn't for you, I wouldn't be saying 'I do' right here, right now. I love you, and I vow to tell you that every single minute of every single day, whether that be with my eyes, my words or my fingertips."

And then she said this to finish her monologue.

"Also, Freddie, I am going to kill you for making me go on that boat across here. You know I had a panic attack just watching *Moana* with Niall and Jessie. But I guess the fact I did it, means I love you just a little bit, right?"

Every single guest burst into laughter, Posy just had a way of bringing tears to everyone's eye with her quick-witted humour.

We both gazed at each other, our eyes reading one another's movements and smiles passing between us that uttered meanings, without anyone else knowing what we were doing.

Eyes for me are a real decider in knowing whether someone truly loves you, and if you truly love them.

You can see the depths of someone through their eyes alone, and when you know what has caused them to cry both for happiness and for sadness, you become an expert at reading and communicating magical things with them.

Never be afraid of looking into someone's eyes and smiling if you feel something there between you. I know I'd regret it if I hadn't, because Posy wouldn't be a part of my life if I'd have kept my head down, and my eyes shut to the beauty right there in front of me.

Andy read out the mandatory wedding recital and within a few moments we were joined as one. Two last minute, awfully cheap silver rings on each of our fingers. It just shows that money doesn't make happiness real, love has a hell of a lot more to do with that.

Posy smiled at me, her cheekbones shimmering under a cloudy sky, brightening up my life – though she had brightened up my life since the day she met me if I'm being honest. She had auspicious (wow, I'm quite proud that I just used that big word, though I am now married to an English Teacher I suppose), brown eyes that told stories that I could listen to over and over again, and her lips were always mesmerizing to me. I couldn't quite believe that I'd have the pleasure of waking up next to such a beautiful soul, from that day on.

We kissed and then I pulled away ever so softly, saying "Hey Mrs. Bayer; I don't think I'll ever get bored of hearing that."

And then all of our friends and family rushed towards us, wooing and throwing sparkles over us, and I couldn't stop smiling. Literally, I am still smiling now as I write this, and I know I always will be, because Posy and I will never have to say goodbye until the day one of us pops off. I hope I either go before her, or on the same day, because I can't imagine myself living without her.

It's good to be humourous about death, especially when you've been loved until your very last day by a person that you know will love you for eternity.

~

Gripping onto Posy's hand which I had grown so familiar to holding, we made our way back down the aisle – this time together as one. I had asked for Westlife's *"World of Our Own"* to be played as we walked away because I knew she'd been a Westlife fan since her teenage years, after a secret chat with Jodie. Jodie had even told me that in Posy's diary she had once found Posy's dream wedding... and the song for her walk down the aisle had indeed been Westlife.

I got to look after my lady's needs, right?

It felt unreal, knowing I'd just married someone that I thought at one point I would never ever find. We had both turned one another's worlds upside down, and I preferred living upside down with her. She reminded me so much of my own Mum. She had her eyes. And her loving heart. She made the world such a beautiful place, full of love and happiness. And she was my star, and I was the fallen star that had fell for her bright soul.

Chapter 28

POSY

The party will never, ever end

After the unforgettable ceremony had come to an end, we made our way to the next adventure... the after party. The heavens opened just after we had said "I Do" and up went those yellow umbrellas.

Then over we went to the makeshift *Gatsby's* bar, which even had a jukebox. I remember feeling like a girl who was loved and not bought.

As Freddie took me in through the doorway, I pulled him close and cried into his chest.

"Baby, what is it, don't you like it?"

"No, no, god Freddie of course I do. It's just that I

don't know how I managed to get you... You're like that fictional guy in every book that every girl dreams they will one day find, and for a while I just never thought I would find my hero. But I did. And I wouldn't change it for anything."

He placed each hand on each of my cheeks and kissed me softly before saying, "If you don't know how lucky you are then I can't even begin to explain how thankful I am for being blessed with you, little lady."

~

Just as the lights went down for our first dance, there was a huge power cut and all of the lights blew. We were left in pure darkness. Suddenly, Freddie let go of me and hurried over to his iPod which was plugged into a wireless speaker.

I nearly laughed out loud as *"Dancing in The Dark"* by Bruce Springsteen erupted from the speakers. And I certainly laughed out loud when Fred came up behind me and pinched my bum, knowing full well he had the benefit of the darkness to make me all hot and flustered in front of my family and friends, who were in very close proximity.

After our session of dancing in the dark – literally – everyone erupted onto the dancefloor and the amount of happiness, right there in that moment was extraordinary. There was no alcohol involved and yet we all danced as if we were high as kites, because happiness, if you let it, can have that same euphoric effect.

Tunes by *The Summer Set* and KC and *The Sunshine Band* blasted from the speakers and we even had a debut from *The Rainer's* with a booty wiggle from Fred in his very tight trousers, which did the job for me.

Pregnancy added to my usual over the top horniness. Lucky Fred. Or poor Fred perhaps – being at my beckon call for the remaining months of my pregnancy.

Jodie and I boogied to our high school hits and Dymphna and I did our dutiful Irish dancing, both looking like absolute nutjobs attempting to look as if we belonged on the *Royal Variety*.

Fred and Noah did some sexy stripper dancing to Marvin Gaye, and the sexy stripper dancing soon came to an end when Noah's pants split after he attempted to challenge the *how low can you go* of DJ Caspar. Boys, eh.

I felt a burst of relief knowing that Noah really might not have been here, and that for one made that night extra special. Like I've said before, love makes many forgettable occurrences unforgettable.

Life moves so fast that sometimes we forget to pause and think, life would be nothing without you.

So, it's worth pausing, if only for a fraction of a second, to remind yourselves of those that love you and those that you love, because otherwise you might one-day regret not taking the time to.

We had heaps of food, which I puked up most of. Pregnancy's such fun sometimes. But it didn't stop me from enjoying every single second. In fact, it reminded me of how happy I was and would be because of Freddie, my family, my friends, and the little peanut inside of me.

Jodie caught my bouquet… ironically, hours later, she and Natalie got drunkenly engaged of course.

Fred was looking so fricking sexy too, all my pregnancy brain could think of was how I could manage to undo his bulging trousers as soon as possible.

Knowing full well that I was wanting sex, Fred kept dancing right up next to me, teasing me with what I wanted.

"Two can play that game." I had whispered in his ear naughtily pushing back into him with my bulging chest – again, thank *you* pregnancy.

But really, two can't play that game when really all those two want to do is tango.

God, he excited me every time he touched me, or looked me in the eye. We did try to go and find a room in the little café at one point because we both couldn't wait much longer, but we were interrupted by Jessie and Niall knocking on the door requesting that me and Uncle Freddie come and dance with them.

Melted my heart, even though I wanted to curse at the little devils!

I suppose I would have to get used the interruptions seeing as I had one of those little blessed devils growing inside of me.

Harvey came and danced with me and it was literally the cutest thing ever. He was wiggling his little hips and spinning me around and around. I knew where Freddie had got his gentlemanly characteristics from.

Everyone I wanted to be there, was. And everything I had ever wanted was captured in that jolly little room. Pure magic.

Jodie was the right kind of tipsy when she started telling us all the funniest of stories. One being how she'd once purchased a pair of vibrating knickers, which had started going off randomly whilst she was showing clients around a potential house. Then she let us in on some news that really made my day even better...

Chapter 29

JODIE

Un-bloody-believable

Posy and Freddie's wedding day was beyond gorgeous and spending it with Natalie by my side made me suddenly want to get married. Hence why I just decided to propose to Nat at the after party. I knew we fitted like two peas in a pod and it just felt right, and good. When I got down on my knees and asked the big question, I think Posy's Nana almost died of shock. Poor thing. She thinks lesbians can spread lesbian disease and make everyone lesbians.

God help us all.

I still can't believe Posy got knocked up before she got married. I mean, I'm supposed to be the reckless, slutty one.

My little Posy – having a miracle baby thanks to Freddie's powerful and feisty sperm! Woo!

I am way too excited to be able to be crazy Aunty Jodie, but Posy has warned me not to be so potty-mouthed when her little one comes along. She's convinced their first word is going to be "Fuck" if I don't start being less expletive. I might just teach him/her that just to annoy her. That's what friends are for, right?

Sometimes I look at Posy, and I see my Dad. A fighter.

I don't think I would have made it through losing him if it wasn't for her. She made it all seem like a mountain I could climb up and not fall from. In many ways, though I lost him, he made sure that I had a loving replacement. Posy.

I still have a picture stuck to my bedroom wall of Posy, her head fluffy and tufty with bits of hair and me hugging her so tight. It was a week after I lost my Dad and Noah had taken it of us at the hospital. It had been the first time since losing him that I had returned to the white-washed ward. Posy made it all okay once again, she helped me get through the impossible, and I came out fighting and living in the moment. I have a lot to thank her for. I'm often too busy goofing around that I forget to stop and think about how fortunate I am to be surrounded with people who I love so much, it's unreal.

~

Just guess who was at Posy's Wedding? And just guess who invited her?

Answer A: Bitch Judith (AKA Hamilton's Mother)

Answer B: Posy's Mum

When I walked down the aisle to go and stand with Nat, Niall and Jessie, I saw her from the corner of my eye. Bitch Judith was stood wearing some sort of pastry hat on her Margaret Thatcher hairstyle. Her face looked as if she was trying to squeeze out a fart. Probably all the Botox...

Boy did she have some fucking nerve showing up at her ex-daughter in laws wedding. I mean, who the fuck even does that?

The truth was, I knew a lot more about the real Bitch Judith than anybody else stood on that mezzanine. I had kept it a secret for way too long, and it was Posy who eventually got it out of me.

~

Come meet me at 2:30. Hubby out. Need u.

My phone flashed with her message whilst I was in the middle of a real estate meeting. I was dealing with my prick of a manager at the time who was trying to get me to sell a property for less than it was worth, for a quick sale.

"No fucking way, I sell my way!" is what I had replied and he went rather white and chose not to mess with me on that day. It's a real concern how I never got fired from that place. So, I quickly finished up the meeting, and didn't sell the property for less than it was worth, and rushed over too Tunbridge Wells - which translates to the poshest fucking area of Kent there is.

I let myself into her house through the back door, making sure no neighbors were around. She kissed me straight away and then dragged me upstairs to her bedroom.

~

I didn't even like the woman, she was vile, bitchy and snotty. And she never hit the spot as it were, but then again, from what Posy had always said, her son couldn't tell clitoris from pelvis either.

I'll admit, our little setup was risky, and mainly for her benefit but I thrived off the thrill of it.

It was Bitch Judith who had come on to me one evening.

It had been a big do for Hamilton's 24th birthday, held at her house, and Posy had gone up to rest in one of the guest rooms because she was practically in a food coma, and the men had gone to the pub.

It was just me and Bitch Judith in the kitchen washing up.

By the way, those are literally the most sexist sentences I have ever wrote – why the fuck was I washing up and not downing a pint at the pub?

Anyway, this was when it all got very weird.

Bitch Judith came up behind me whilst I was washing up leftovers in the sink and whispered in my ear, "I know this is wrong, but I want you."

I was just like what the actual hell is going on right now...

Then it had all just happened, in her room, next to the one Posy was fast asleep in. It was silly and it was stupid.

I have no idea to this day how Bitch Judith figured out I was gay. Nobody knew my sexuality until my relationship with Natalie. But they do say that there is such a thing as 'gaydar'. And Bitch Judith sure had it.

Over our next couple of secret sessions, Bitch Judith confided in me that she would never be able to be with me fully because she didn't want her husband, nor anybody else to find out about her 'lesbian tendencies'.

She told me that since she was in high school she knew she was gay but her Mother had always told her that 'all homosexuals are sinners' and the rest of the bull crap.

Like I've said, we kept up our secret affair for a good few months, that was until she publicly offended Posy, directly in front of me. And besides, if you hurt a friend of mine, you are no friend.

Posy had been enthusiastically telling Bitch Judith, me and Hamilton about her plans to travel abroad and take a year out of teaching. I was fully supportive of it. I was, after all, the reckless *live everyday as if it's your last* kind of friend.

Bitch Judith had stared at Posy, her eyes as cutting a fox before slyly and pedantically saying.

"You know dear. You're not really fit for international travel. Especially not on that teacher wage of yours. Besides, you should be at home cleaning and taking care of the home seeing as you can't do a proper wife's job of having my son's kids."

I know what you're thinking. *No fucking way did she just say that shit.*

But she did. And Hamilton just stood there nodding like the sodding little weed he is.

And on that day our lesbian affair or whatever it is you want to call it ended for good. I walked out of her house and gave her a finger (different to the ones I'd been giving her on previous meetings), before telling her that she had no right to treat any human like she had just treated her daughter in law.

~

When I saw her standing amongst the guests, I guess that's when I decided that I was going to come clean about it all. Posy deserved to know.

So, after downing a few whiskeys that I had snuck into my handbag at the afterparty, I got talking to Posy. Posy was trying not to let Bitch Judith being there ruin her day, she was after all one of her Mum's closest friends and so didn't want to make a scene. Besides, she had said, "At least Hamilton isn't here. I think Fred would have rugby tackled him, and then disconnected his nuts from his body."

That's when I had said, "Look Posy, I have something to tell you that I should have told you ages ago."

She looked at me searching for an answer in my face, which was by this point smirking.

Bitch Judith had sworn me to secrecy but she kind of deserved a bit of her own medicine, right? Besides, I had one of those urges to tell Posy there and then for fear of never having the balls to tell her again. I think it was the whisky doing the talking, but I needed to clear the air of the past with my best friend.

"So, I'm not the only lesbian in the room tonight." I blurted out.

Posy had pointed at Nat, questioning my statement, confused at what I was trying to tell her. I was a bit tipsy to be fair, it's no surprise she looked at me like I was just drunkenly rambling. I grabbed Posy's finger and pointed it towards Bitch Judith, who was stood just yards away.

Bitch Judith's eyes by this point practically exploded from her head. She could just about hear our conversation from where she was standing.

"Bitch Judith is in fact also Lesbian Judith." I told Posy, my voice slurring with the whisky courage.

"Oh, give over Jodie, you've had way too much to drink Mrs., stop being silly!" Posy told me, giggling.

But my face stayed completely pokerfaced.

"Oh my god. are you being serious? You *are* actually being serious, aren't you? Oh my god, tell me Jodie, tell me for god's sakes!" Posy questioned, her hands reaching for her cheeks in astonishment and shock.

"Yup. And I can tell you first hand she's just as bad in the pussy department as her own son."

Posy burst out laughing, her chuckles erupting from her so loudly that by this point Bitch Judith began walking over to us, well, more like storming over. She was like a tomato with her crimson cheeks burning right up.

To exacerbate the situation further I stood up on my chair and shouted over to Freddie who was in control of the iPod Docking station, "I've got a song request, *'I Kissed a Girl'* by Katy Perry. It's Judith's favourite!"

Chapter 30

NOAH

That's Life

I don't know where to start, or how to explain to you how happy I am. Freddie worked his magic on his wedding day and made sure that Nancy was there.

I think we had both come to our senses and realized the extent of our situation, and the reality attached to it. There were a few tears, then one of the longest hugs known to man and a cheeky kiss.

Throughout Posy's wedding day, Nancy aided me in getting out of my wheelchair for a little dance, and then telling me when I needed to rest. She cared for me, and I cared for her.
Nancy and I had something so precious, and I really do believe that fate brought us together. The same

type of fate that Freddie and Posy, and Nat and Jodie were brought together by.

Strangely, before I had met Nancy I had always brushed off fate as some sort of fantasy excuse for bad and good things happening to people. But when I met Nancy I finally believed in the idea that sometimes two people are put back together, like a jigsaw, because they are meant to make a beautiful masterpiece. Sure, sometimes pieces went missing and things fell apart, but the view was still mesmerizing.

When the hospital found out about our romance, the entire ward went wild applauding and shouting out "At LAST!" ... apparently there had been a betting pot for when we would get together. I hadn't realized that others had seen what I had seen all along. Love.

Nancy and I took things super slowly. And I mean like turtle pace. First it began as coffee dates out at various little urban coffees, and then she would come along to walk Bob with me, so that we could spend some quiet time together, just talking and also so that she could make sure that I was building in strength – she said that caring for my wellbeing was, after all, her job.

I waited a while before I properly introduced Nancy to Jessie and Niall. Not because I was unsure if they would like her, because I *knew* that they would like her. She was kind, sweet and caring. Basically, everything that their mother had never been.

The first time Nancy and I slept together was absolutely hilarious. Not only did my arm cramp up because of its utter uselessness with the nerve damage from the crash, but it cramped up whilst I was... well... I think you can infer what I'm getting at here!

Nancy was so good about it. I was so unbelievably embarrassed, but she was so lighthearted about it. So loving and caring. She was like Nancy from *Oliver Twist*. Kindhearted, loved by all and beautiful in every movement she made.

I'm thinking of asking her to marry me. Jessie and Niall have been pondering me for months. One day, after all of this Izzy nonsense is over, Nancy is going to be my one, forever.

I want her to be a part of me indefinitely.

~

My divorce with Izzy is still going through the courts as we speak. It seems Hamilton has been giving her some tips towards handling a divorce settlement, because she is trying her hardest to claim that she wasn't ever having an affair.

Posy was more than happy to be a witness to the

court, and was of course as explicit as she could possibly be.

It'll soon be over. Divorce isn't something I ever imagined myself going through. From a young age, I told myself how I was going to only ever have one true love, and stay with that person forever.
I guess Izzy had been my blip before I found my true love, Nancy. Though I'm not exactly best friends with Izzy these days, I certainly don't regret our time together. Sure, there were bad memories, fallouts and difficulties but I got two of the best gifts from our marriage – Jessie and Niall. Now they are two people I could never live without. They bring a lot of love into life, and laughter too, every single day. They are both growing up so quickly, and cannot wait to meet their new cousin... whenever he or she may arrive!

~

Right now, I'm not really sure how my medical state is going to affect my future. My memory is rapidly improving and I go to the memory clinic every two weeks. I read somewhere once that sometimes a new love can bring your brain waves back to life. Thank god for Nancy.

My arm is forever going to be dodgy, the doctors have told me that it may well build in strength, but it's unlikely that I'll ever get full use of it back. My back, however, is very nearly back to its original state. Apparently, I am a walking miracle.

Regarding the crash, the driver, Nancy's brother, is serving ten years in prison.

I've forgiven him over the whole ordeal, I am after all still here, and also through the crash, I met Nancy.
Sure, it's probably one of the shittiest, most unluckiest parts of my life so far but I've made it through it all, and I've come out the other end a happier and stronger person. I still get to see my kids every day and I have the most incredible bond with Bob because he is my little helper. I try to approach it in the most positive way and Nancy has been a big help in my being able to move on from the past and face the future of us.

~

Posy and Freddie absolutely adored returning to Barcelona and visiting India for the first time for their honeymoon, which I had organised. And they could not put into words how amazing India had been.

Both Posy and Freddie had gotten Delhi Belly in its purest form and Posy cursed me over the phone one evening because her morning sickness was coming out of one end, and her Delhi Belly the other. She's always been so very blunt and unbelievably hilarious. My sister.

I remember when I was a teenager and seeing sisters as being super annoying, whiny and hormonal. But now, I respect Posy and I love her to pieces. I'm glad she's found someone that truly cares for her needs, and not their own. It seems we both married the wrong people, but luckily the right ones found us eventually.

I am super excited to be an Uncle. I never thought I would be. I knew Posy's medical history and I had accepted it. When she and Freddie came around following their honeymoon to tell us all the news I nearly fainted with shock.

Not only had I gotten a new brother, which was the most unexpected miracle, but I was also going to be something I never thought I would be. It was a truly crazy year. Life changes so rapidly and surprises us constantly.

When we had all been told the baby news, Jessie and Niall insisted on both lying with their heads on Posy's tummy. When they felt the baby kicking they both screamed so loud that Bob began running around in circles and barking. He's such a little nutcase. He must have some of Posy's genes... Ha-ha! She's gonna kill me if she ever reads this.

~

I'm not working right now but I am volunteering a few days a week at an Alcoholics Anonymous group.

I provide verbal support and try and share my story. In a way, I feel I'm helping change people who are prepared to face their problem, so that car crashes like the one I was involuntarily involved in, can be less and less common.

At first, I found it pretty hard being in a room with a lot of people who had been issued with several drunk driving offences. But I eventually got to know them and their stories, and almost respected them for getting help before it was too late.

We all make mistakes and they do change us as a person, but we shouldn't let them define who we are or who we want to be. Facing our mistakes is a respectable quality – being ashamed of them isn't going to change your life for the better, you have to rise above them and use them to make yourself a stronger person.

Nancy keeps telling me that I should get into public speaking with my newfound positive attitude to life. Perhaps I will one day. That's life – it's unpredictable and you have the choice to own it, and make it yours to live how you want to.

For me, a life with Nancy, Niall, Jessie and Bob is just what I need and what I have always wanted.

Chapter 31

ALFIE

Why did I let her go?

I'll admit it. I was an utter arsehole to Posy. She's always on my mind. I don't really know why I stopped calling; in a way, I got scared because I really loved her. But I didn't deserve her, I knew that.

It's crazy how one girl can change your whole perspective on life. And stay etched onto your heart in marker pen forever, no matter how hard you try and erase her.

The last time I had seen her was the night before she had left for Barcelona. I'm not really sure how that night had happened, she informed me that it was "no strings attached sex" and "just for closure."

It was that last time together where I felt something more than just 'no strings attached'.

The truth is, I've always put my passion for music before girls. I've always used girls when I needed inspiration for my music or when I was feeling lonely. But Posy was different.

I know it sounds crazy because I treated her so bad but if I ever had the chance, I would hold her so tight and never let her go. I would take back every bad thing I had ever said to her, and take away all of the hurt. She didn't deserve any of it.

I've grown up a lot since those mistakes I made. She changed me. She was also the best sex I have ever had.

Our bodies used to rock together so melodically, like the black and white keys of a piano, working in unison to create a sweet song. Our love was passionate and hectic and it scared the shit out of me. It still scares the shit out of me when I think of the effect she used to have on me, when we were dating all those months ago.

Sometimes it feels like years ago since we were making love against my piano, and sometimes it feels like yesterday. If only I hadn't run away like a little boy, that magical bond we had might have become something even more spell binding.

She enchanted me with her charm, quick-witted humour and outstanding beauty. Why did I let her go?

~

I never intended on moving back to England but after Posy, I needed a fresh start, something to get my mind off her.

I moved back home to Surrey and took a job in the local shop. Whilst I was abroad I had been able to teach without a formal teaching qualification so I knew that at some point I would need to take a year to qualify, when I returned to the UK. A customer informed me of the need for teachers in Kent and the paid scholarships available. They were frankly desperate for teachers of all subjects. And so, I applied.

Never in a million years did I think I'd get placed in a school where Posy used to work before she set off travelling. It was truly crazy.

It got even crazier when news spread that Posy was going to be returning to the school. My heart didn't have a clue what it was about to be faced with.

Chapter 32

POSY

The last chapter

Leaving the wedding after-party venue, with everyone cheering and waving us off, we made our way to the Corvette waiting outside; we climbed into the back seat and kissed each other as if on cue.

Me in my blush pink, extraordinary, rockabilly bridal gown, and Freddie armed with his red blazer and cropped, seamlessly skin-tight trousers. It felt so right, like something you couldn't even dream about, nor put down in words.

And by *it,* I mean the feeling inside of me... oh good god, there's no way of trying to explain it without sounding like an utter sex addict.

Though, speaking truthfully it took a lot of self-control not to just grab hold of Fred right there and then, seeing as we had the audience of the driver in front and no partition... damn!

I mean, who doesn't love car sex? Though not particularly practical when you own a Mini! FYI!

I did however tease him a little bit by whispering a little something in his ear... but that's not for you to hear either. Let's just say it's probably the phrase that got me pregnant!

I had presumed the driver was taking us home, but I noticed I was wrong almost immediately as I noticed him head onto the motorway, leading us back to the airport.

"This was all Noah's idea," Freddie said, his gleeful smile creeping through his poker face.

"He knew we'd met in Barcelona and when I rang him this morning to tell him the news he asked if he could organize the honeymoon... so he booked us two tickets. We're honeymooning *Eat, Pray, Love* style, because after Barcelona, we're going to India too."

I literally squealed with excitement. Whaaaaaattttt!!! My brother was such a little secret-keeper.

"He's packed our luggage with the help of Jodie and Nat, and he's wrote you a letter to read before you get on the plane," Fred said, passing over a scrappy little note written in Noah's typical boy writing.

I was buzzing so much with the news that my hands were literally shaking, as I opened the letter up:

Dear Posy,

In life, you find people that you never dreamed of finding, and for me that's you. And for you, that's now Freddie.

You've been my best friend since the beginning and I couldn't imagine a day without you. You are one of a kind in every way, and a tad bit eccentric – but hey, my kids love that about their crazy Aunt Posy.

I know I won't really be able to travel much with my memory and dodgy arm, but I want you to, for me.

I hope you have a safe flight, and maybe even join the Mile-High Club… and feel free to keep that type of information to yourself.

You two are officially the perfect strangers, and I love you both dearly.

Hope you get a nice tan in Barcelona.

Also, hope you don't get the shits in India.

Your big bro, Noah x

I didn't know whether to laugh or cry. God, I had the best two men in my life... like, ever.

First, we were going to be back to our beautiful Barcelona and then we were flying to India... frickin India!!!

I was literally too excited to even speak. I'd got engaged, told Fred I was pregnant, got married and was going to Barcelona all on the same day. I frankly was close to peeing my pants with utter anticipation, and with the baby using my bladder as a bouncy castle that was making it all much worse!

I couldn't help but kiss Freddie's lips like it was the last time, because I loved him as if it was.

~

Our time on the airport passed by quickly as we walked around the terminal, both dressed in our wedding gear, and both in awe of how surreal the past few months had been. The paparazzi kept jumping out from various shops dotted around the airport, but we were in our own little bubble.

And gee, the sexual tension was making us both ache.

Security had been tightened as they knew Freddie would be travelling and so with beady eyes on us, there was no chance of escaping to consummate the marriage...

That was until we got on the plane. And all was dark. And everyone else on the plane was sensibly asleep.

Freddie had innocently gone to the bathroom, not having known my intention or Noah's discrete encouragement to do what I did.

I got up from the cushioned airplane seat, and made my way to the back of the plane. Sneaking inside the toilet partition just as Freddie was opening it was some *James Bond* type of shit... I was smooth.

Kissing him, making his lips hurt I took him by surprise, as he fumbled for the lock on the door.

"Well hello there Mrs Bayer." He had breathlessly said, kissing me passionately up against the sink.

"I couldn't wait any longer!" I squealed, gasping as he kissed me along my jawline and trailed his soft fingers along my neck.

And then I suddenly got the giggles.

"Oh my god, you know what I was just thinking?" I said, unable to hide my laughter. Fred looked at me intrigued and eager for more of me.

"This is like that scene on *Snakes on Plane* when the snake falls out of the toilet roof and grabs right onto the guy's..."

We were both crying with laughter, especially when Freddie leant on the toilet flush and nearly fell down the toilet. Why are airplane toilets so fucking tiny? They should cater for two. Me and the baby I mean... Ha-ha!

He kissed me more and more urgently, as we both undressed one another, giggling as we heard a young child outside demanding, "Mummy I need a BIG poo!" followed by him stomping around shouting, "Poo poo poo!" and banging on the door.

And kissing me as he made me climax with one last final push I truly understood the true concept of love making. So many people go on about shagging and fucking and whatever other synonyms they use these days, but that was love. It was two people rocking gently together, enjoying one another, made for one another. Also, I can now tick the Mile-High certificate off my bucket list. As can Freddie.

Besides, who can claim to having their first marital sex on a plane to Barcelona – that's going to be a great story to tell.

As we exited the airplane bathroom, both red from the embarrassment of having to face the little boy who needed a big poo, we both had to sit and wait for two more hours until we landed.

Both of us were throbbing for more of one another, but knew we would need to get some sleep before landing.

Freddie, my husband, turned to me, his sexy glow on his face and whispered, "I love you Posy Bayer, and I love Baby Bayer already too."

I looked at him, transfixed and mesmerized by his sheer effect on me, and at the pure beauty of knowing inside me was something that symbolized us.

Recalling on the reunion of us, I snuggled into Freddie and said, "I still can't believe you wrote a song about me," then paused, thoughtfully before concluding, "I feel like I need to do something in return…"

I kissed him softly on the cheek before saying a sentence that he'll never forget.

"Who knows, maybe I'll write a book about you."

~

Settling back into my hometown with Freddie was like a dream. He went off on tour every couple of weeks, and flew back more than he should to come and see me and have amazing sex.

I didn't get jealous of him being surrounded by thousands of girls in stilettos. I trusted him with every part of me and loved him more than I can explain in words.

I got my job back at Kent Grange High for the remainder of my pregnancy, and the kids all cheered when I walked back into my little room, decorated with flowers and memories of the past. Apparently, I'd been the talk of the school when news had gotten round that I was returning. It warmed by heart.

In other news, Hamilton is no longer with his abnormally hairy bonking device (AKA Izzy), but I hear he is with some new Victoria Beckham lookalike. Jodie told me that she saw Hamilton in Morrison's the other week and he was wearing what looked like women's cutoff, ripped, pink jeans. Talk about a mid-life crisis. Jodie had also sent me picture proof via Snapchat and made his head into a penis using the drawing tool. She's so hilarious.

Noah is still as lovely as ever, the best Daddy ever, and in a relationship with his Nurse friend. Oooohhh aye. They're FACEBOOK OFFICIAL. That is some serious shit. They are truly so unbelievably cute together and they just get each other, you know?

Nat and Jodie are also planning on eloping to Singapore to get married in a bar called *Jigger and Pony* (which I'm told is one of the best gay bars in Singapore). What else would you expect from Jodie? She's a nutter. Love her to bits.

~

But my life has changed unexpectedly. In two ways.

The other day I was asked to observe one of the new trainee Art History teachers. I walked into the classroom and there stood Alfie Dalton.

Yes, I could not fucking believe it either.

The guy who my world had revolved around at one point, who had broken my heart and joined the long list of douchebags I had previously dated.

My heart was confused.

And then suddenly I did some math's in my head, staring down at my bump and staring at Alfie who had just clocked me and my big bump.

The doctors had kept telling me I was much bigger than an expected three-month bump.

Shit, Alfie was the last person I had slept with before Freddie... could it be his? Please no. No way, it couldn't be. Surely not...

And as I took a seat at the back of the classroom, still unable to face the reality of the situation, I also felt a wet sensation between my legs, and that is when I heard a student scream, "Miss, you're bleeding!"

~

And now I don't know who or what this book is

about, but I do know that my story is about to change drastically.

I see blue and red lights. And then, black.

Praise for *I Wrote A Book About You:*

'Lovely and totally different'
Dave Lane, Author

'The relatable misfortunes of Posy make this a brilliant read for all of the ladies. Heartwarming, and real, with a hilarious girl-mance to top it off'
Bobbie Buchanan

'Fab storyline and great characters'
Emily Hart

'Beautifully written'
Carole Thomas

'I did actually spit out coffee as I guffawed at one of the many one liners and quips'
Nicole Strange

'A definite full 5 stars'
Vicky Haslam

'Her writing skills are outstanding!'
Zoe Smith

Press and Social Media for Amy Louise Ware, Author of 'I Wrote A Book About You'

Email: ALWareBooks@gmail.com

Facebook Pages:

https://www.facebook.com/IWroteABookAboutYou/
https://www.facebook.com/AmyLouiseWareBOOKS/

Twitter:

@ALWareBooks

Instagram:

@amylouiseware

If you enjoyed reading this novel, please tell all of your friends about it, and get in touch via any of the above ways. Amy loves hearing her readers' views on her novels!

Reviews on Amazon are always welcome!

Why not help spread the word about #IWABAY by taking a picture of you with your copy and sending it to the author at ALWareBooks@gmail.com...

Thank you!

Printed in Great Britain
by Amazon